THE CTHULHU WARS

THE UNITED STATES' BATTLES AGAINST THE MYTHOS

BY KENNETH HITE AND
KENNON BAUMAN

ILLUSTRATIONS DARREN TAN

First published in Great Britain in 2016 by Osprey Publishing,
PO Box 883, Oxford, OX1 9PL, UK
1385 Broadway, 5th Floor, New York, NY 10018, USA

E-mail: info@ospreypublishing.com

Osprey Publishing is part of Bloomsbury Publishing Plc

A CIP catalog record for this book is available from the British Library.

Print ISBN: 978 1 4728 0787 8
PDF e-book ISBN: 978 1 4728 0788 5
EPUB e-book ISBN: 978 1 4728 0789 2

Typeset in Adobe Garamond Pro, Bank Gothic, Conduit and American Typewriter
Originated by PDQ Media, Bungay, UK
Printed in China through World Print Ltd.

16 17 18 19 20   10 9 8 7 6 5 4 3 2 1

CONTENTS

INTRODUCTION

The greatest challenge to the historian, I think, is the difficulty of correlating all the contents relevant to a given event. We can assemble a reasoned picture of a given battle or biography in the midst of the black seas of obscurity, but in many cases it is not allowed that we should voyage too far. In the case of the American military campaigns against the so-called "Cthulhu Mythos," a shadow of secrecy remains over all but a few operations. These operations, each superficially unconnected to the larger war, have been exposed or publicized under very different lights – including propaganda and outright fiction. However, I am confident that in the future some scholar will piece this dissociated knowledge together and open up the true vista of the conflict, and of the United States' central position therein. On that day, the historical establishment shall either shoulder its true responsibility to humanity, or flee from the deadly light of research and evidence into the peace and safety of "skepticism" and "debunking" of "dangerous blends of fact and fiction."

The unpalatable truth of the matter is that there is not, as yet, sufficient historically valid material to write, or even outline, a definitive chronicle of the United States' quarter-millennium of war against the Cthulhu Mythos – or, to use the current preferred jargon, "coordinated national effort to investigate and contain phenomena involving *Necronomicon*-Related Entities (NREs)." It remains something of an embarrassment to the military historian that the primary source of information on the nature of the enemy is a series of pulp fiction stories written by Howard Phillips Lovecraft (1890–1937), an eccentric New England fantasist. True, in many cases Lovecraft based his tales on solid research and documentary evidence. His numerous trips to the area around Arkham, Massachusetts have been conclusively mapped by his biographers, and his "Borrowing Privileges" card from Miskatonic University's Orne Library can be viewed among his personal papers in the John Hay Library at Brown even after three separate "national security redactions" of the material. Lovecraft had an immense circle of personal correspondence, including not just fellow authors but also scientists, anthropologists, and government officials: however, many of these letters have vanished into the archives of the Multi-Agency Joint Intelligence Command (MAJIC), which has directed the Cthulhu Wars since 1947. Even from the little that remains, it is clear that many of Lovecraft's correspondents considered him not only a clearing-house for comparing notes, but also an authority on the enigmas they encountered in their careers and a safe channel for judicious leaks.

That said, Lovecraft undeniably drew many of the proper names and entire scenes in his tales not from academic papers or suppressed after-action reports but from his own nightmares. His dreams had been remarkably detailed and specific since childhood, and his habit of recording them shortly after waking has been shown in psychological studies to be an excellent method of strengthening and intensifying dream recall. In his fictions, of course, Cthulhu and other NREs manifest and communicate in dreams – in the ongoing war, Lovecraft's dreams may actually be the equivalent of a scouting mission or code-breaking effort, voluntary or not. Certainly one of Lovecraft's primary fictional alter egos, Randolph Carter, deliberately explores occult mysteries both in and out of deliberately induced dream states. But as that example indicates, treating Lovecraft's fictions as front-line war reporting or tactical intelligence is likely as dangerous as ignoring them entirely: unlike Randolph Carter, the US military, for example, is unlikely ever to have assembled an army of talking cats for dream-wars on the Moon. Lovecraft deliberately changed, conflated, or contracted many names, locations, and events to improve the tales as fiction.

The best we can do, then, is use the fiction as a background: one into which may be inserted the few provable details of the war, and against which we may infer certain larger movements and shapes. Military secrecy and national security measures forbid us further information, and prevent us from knowing for certain whether (or how much of) our inference is valid. If Lovecraft's fictions are to be taken as gospel, this shroud of ignorance may itself be a legitimate war–fighting measure revealing the truth of the Mythos supposedly drives men and nations mad. But sooner or later, a democracy must learn the truth about its own defenses or fail internally and externally.

Who knows the end? What has been published may be classified, but what was closed may be opened. The US military fights and perhaps dreams in the deep, and knowledge spreads through whispers and Internet alike. Some have advised me not to complete this manuscript, worrying that it, and I, will vanish into some nameless prison. Perhaps that time will come – but I cannot believe it! But let me pray that, if I do not survive this book, my publishers may put truth before caution and see that it meets as many eyes as possible.

–Kenneth Hite, 2014

Although H. P. Lovecraft had no direct demonstrable connection to the various covert operations against the Mythos, his life between 1908 and 1913 – from the ages of 18 to 23 – is an almost complete blank. During that time, Inspector Legrasse may have recruited Lovecraft into his ring of unofficial investigators of the Cthulhu cult, perhaps initially as a researcher into New England folklore. This work could have inspired his uncannily accurate "fiction" – and perhaps also triggered post-traumatic stress later in life. (Pictorial Press Ltd./ Alamy)

I have done what I could to assemble a clear and sensible text from the scattered notes and outlines recovered from Kenneth Hite's home, adding detail where possible from the partially redacted and declassified government documents he received as the result of his apparently quite numerous Freedom of Information Act (FOIA) requests. Every reasonable effort has been made to preserve Mr Hite's conclusions, at least insofar as they were clearly stated: his last writings were, quite frankly, barely comprehensible. It is an incredible shame that the fire took him and his magnificent library so suddenly, but it seems, in examining his papers, that he was not well when he passed. Still, no one (outside the Pentagon, at least) knew more about this subject than Kenneth Hite. I hope my meager attempt to bring his last and greatest work to light is a fitting tribute to a man I considered a friend.

–Kennon Bauman, 2015

THREAT REPORT: NRES

"They worshipped the Great Old Ones who lived ages before there were any men, and who came to the young world out of the sky. Those Old Ones were gone now, inside the earth and under the sea; but their dead bodies had told their secrets in dreams to the first men, who formed a cult which had never died. This was that cult, and it had always existed and always would exist, hidden in distant wastes and dark places all over the world until the time when the great priest Cthulhu, from his dark house in the mighty city of R'lyeh under the waters, should rise and bring the earth again beneath his sway. Some day he would call, when the stars were ready, and the secret cult would always be waiting to liberate him."

—summary of prisoner interrogations from the St. Bernard Parish Raid, 1907

It can be difficult to wage a war if you cannot identify your enemies. The various cults, grimoires, dreams, and *romans-à-clef* from which the US tries to sift strategic intelligence in the Cthulhu Wars contradict themselves mightily, sometimes within the same page of fiction or scripture. The term "Old Ones," for example, can mean the monstrosities attending Cthulhu, the class of titanic entities including Cthulhu, or the crinoid aliens that warred against Cthulhu during the Paleozoic Era. Similarly, the term "Cthulhu Mythos" refers to the mythological body of lore around the beings, not the beings themselves.

Rather than parse insane or extraterrestrial theology, the US military now uses the general term *Necronomicon-Related Entities* (NREs) to refer to "unique, titanic beings of this or any other dimension, referenced either in the *Necronomicon* or in texts interrelated with it." (Military and MAJIC personnel also use NRE as an adjective when referring to anomalous phenomena, "servitor" or other species, or anything else associated with these beings, although "Mythos" is also a common descriptor.) The *Necronomicon,* or *al-Azif* to use its original Arabic name, is a blasphemous "anti-Scripture" written around 730 by the Yemeni mystic and sorcerer Abd al-Azrad (655?–738), called "Alhazred" in medieval European texts such as *De Vermis Mysteriis.*

Some of the NREs – Cthulhu, Rhan-Tegoth, and Ghatanothoa, among others – are known to have material existence, and are simply gigantic extraterrestrials rather than spiritually exalted "gods." Others, more traditional gods perhaps, have only been encountered as names and titles in grimoires and recorded cult rituals: Azathoth, the "Blind Idiot Sultan;" Hastur, "The Unnamable One;" Yog-Sothoth, "The Key and the Gate;" and Shub-Niggurath, the "Black Goat of the Woods With a Thousand Young." Alhazredic mythology places some NREs between categories: physical beings dwelling in taboo dimensions ("Outside"), sacred realms ("Yoth"), or (symbolically?) on other planets such as Saturn: for example, Gol-Goroth, Yig, and Tsathoggua, respectively. Perhaps none of the NREs is a true deity, although if a single being can cause planetary extinction, parsing its right to godhood seems irrelevant.

Many NREs, such as Dagon, Mormo, Nodens, and Itlaqqa, exceed mere cultism. They were – and in some cases still are – worshiped as deities by entire populations, which often swaddle the true natures of these outlandish beings in comforting or self-aggrandizing myth. Other NREs were likely worshiped under other names, either as esoteric tradition or by simple linguistic drift: Yig as the Kukulkan of the Maya and Quetzalcoatl of the Aztec, or Cthulhu as the Etruscan god Tuchulcha and the Tongan god Tutula. Nathaniel Wingate Peaslee's controversial works argue that *all* human religions are similar misunderstandings of the nature of the NREs and their activities, identifying (for example) Yahweh with Yog-Sothoth. Shortly after he published his *Traumatic Origins of the Religious Impulse* in 1951, Peaslee lost his MAJIC security clearance, though he (just barely) kept his tenure at Miskatonic University.

ON THE DARK FRONTIER (1585–1815)

"Men, in at least some Corners of the World, and perhaps in such as God may have some special Designs upon, will to their Cost, be more Familiarized with the World of Spirits, than they had been formerly."

–Cotton Mather, *Wonders of the Invisible World*

By the 17th century, most Native American tribes had developed a vast corpus of oral history identifying those lands safe for settlement, passing this knowledge from generation to generation via shamans and elders to ensure that they would continue to maintain their own villages, hunting grounds, and burial places at a safe distance from NRE influence. Only at great peril did they ignore their instinctive need to band together to avoid excessive exposure to the great natural – and unnatural – dangers that lay in the shadows of the North American landscape. The disastrous results of exposure to the truly profane locales poisoned by their long association with NREs reinforced these taboos still more.

The stone circles and megalithic constructions reported in New England marked some of these taboo sites, either as warnings or as channels or both. The Mystery Hill megalithic complex, more popularly known as "America's Stonehenge," in Salem, New Hampshire, is perhaps the best known today. Mystery Hill shares a variety of astronomical alignments and structural similarities with several other megalithic sites scattered across the region, including the Slate Hill complex between Attica and Chorazin,

New York, and in Massachusetts the subterranean tunnel system at Pratt Hill near Upton, the megaliths atop Burnt Hill near Heath, and the Sentinel Hill stones near Dunwich. "Round towers" attested in Newport, Rhode Island, and in the Miskatonic River valley portion of the Hockomock Swamp may be pre-Columbian (possibly Norse) structures, but most likely they date from the early colonial period before the perils of these locations had been realized.

Even after the first waves of European colonization, many of these "NRE-positive" areas remained isolated and untouched. European settlement, in many cases, flowed into former Native territories left depopulated following plagues and wars. Isolated whites met the same fates as isolated Natives: death, madness, or worse. Certain districts were shunned: first for good reason, and then through habit or superstition. As Dr Albert K. Wilmarth put it in his 1924 monograph "Settlement Folkways in Vermont":

> *"The ways of the Vermonters became settled; and once their habitual paths and dwellings were established according to a certain fixed plan, they remembered less and less what fears and avoidances had determined that plan, and even that there had been any fears or avoidances. Most people simply knew that certain hilly regions were considered as highly unhealthy, unprofitable, and generally unlucky to live in, and that the farther one kept from them the better off one usually was. In time the ruts of custom and economic interest became so deeply cut in approved places that there was no longer any reason for going outside them, and the haunted hills were left deserted by accident rather than by design."*

Of course, some of the new colonists came looking for just such haunted hills.

Lost Colonies

In August 1585, 107 English colonists set foot for the first time on an island the local Algonquian-speaking tribes called Roanoke. They built a small fort on the northern end of the island, but remained on Roanoke for less than a year before fleeing to England, complaining of hostile natives and unnatural storms. The sailors of Sir Francis Drake, who evacuated the first colony, "cast overboard … all our Cards, Bookes, and writings" to calm the "boisterous" seas and refloat the pinnaces that had somehow grounded themselves in the treacherous waters.

The site of the Roanoke colony had been chosen sight unseen by Thomas Harriot, an Oxford-educated court astronomer, mathematician, linguist, and navigator – and coincidentally, a protégé of the magus John Dee. Harriot and Dee had mapped the new colony's location in the early 1580s, during the same time that they translated the *Necronomicon* and at the beginning of Dee's period of "angelic" ultra-terrestrial contacts. In 1583, the occult-minded Sir Walter Raleigh may have sent his half-brother Sir Humphrey Gilbert to check Harriot's calculations: Gilbert's expedition spotted a sea monster, then his ship *HMS Squirrel* disappeared in "Pyramid wise" seas.

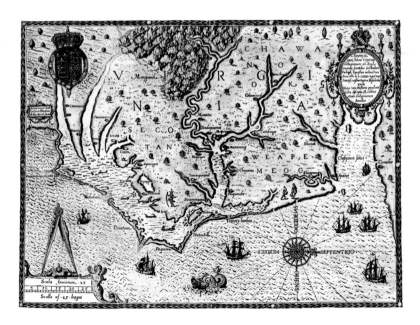

Theodore de Bry engraved this map of the Roanoke area in 1590, based on an original by John White. "Roanoac" is the pink island in the center. By an odd coincidence, the pirate Edward "Blackbeard" Teach (1680?–1718) made his base on Ocracoke Island, unnamed just north of "Croatoan" on this map. Blackbeard returned here in 1718 with a "chest of medicines" seized from Charleston, searching for the sailors' Dreamland "Fiddler's Green" (possibly related to Harriot's "green meadow" Stethelos), but quick action by Royal Navy Lieutenant Robert Maynard closed the pirate's Gate. (North Wind Picture Libray / Alamy)

Eyewitnesses on another ship saw Gilbert reading a book on the stern and lifting his palm to the skies as the *Squirrel* went down.

Harriot's calculations had pinpointed a land of "green meadows" he believed to be a reflection of lost Stethelos, an ancient city or country referenced in the Greek *Pnakotika,* an early compilation of Mythos lore supposedly dating to pre-human times. Raleigh organized a second scouting expedition in 1584, and upon its success gave command of the 1585 colonizing expedition to the experienced mariner Sir Richard Grenville; Harriot accompanied one or both of these. Whatever he found there, Harriot returned to England to stay.

Grenville returned to the colony some ten months later with additional supplies, only to find it evacuated. He left a small detachment of soldiers on the island to secure the abandoned fort, and in June 1587 yet another group of colonists arrived. They found Grenville's detachment gone, save for a single human skeleton "of seemingly ancient provenance" clad in tattered but recognizable English garb. Despite these ill tidings, the expedition's commander, a former Portuguese pirate named Simon Fernandez, disembarked 115 new colonists at sword-point before setting sail to return to England.

Whether anyone now knew Raleigh and Harriot's original occult plans for the colony, the Spanish Armada crisis distracted British naval power until August 1590. When colonial governor John White finally returned he found the colony completely dismantled: buildings, tools, and even rudimentary roads gone, as if the entire establishment had simply disappeared. A brief investigation revealed no signs of struggle or violence; indeed, the only clue White discovered was the word "CROATOAN" carved on a tree near the center of the missing settlement. MAJIC gives little credence to the theory deriving this inscription from the Mnari word *kara-itun,* cognate with the Sumerian *garas-iritush,* meaning "catastrophe (or doom) of the city," preferring to derive it from the local Croatan tribe. The name likely derives from *kro-otan,* "speaking town": a meeting place, or perhaps a holy place to hear the voices of local gods or spirits.

A sudden storm forced White's relief fleet away from the island before he could mount a more concerted search, and none of the colonists were ever found.

Places of Dagon

After Roanoke, English colonization set down deeper roots in Virginia and Massachusetts. In 1625, the barrister Thomas Morton built a trading post on an isolated, hilly peninsula along the Atlantic coast just a few miles from the Puritan colony at Plymouth. He named it "Merrymount" or "Mount Ma-re," conflating ecstasy and the sea in a fashion hinting at Deep One contacts, possibly from their nearby colony off Devil Reef.

By 1626, Merrymount had become infamous as the site of heathen ceremonies and disturbing debaucheries performed by English settlers and Native tribesmen alike. According to Plymouth Governor William Bradford's *History of Plymouth Plantation,* the residents of Merrymount set up a ring of stones and an 80ft "May-pole" carved with queer images and topped with deer antlers, "dancing about it many days together … like so many fairies, or furies rather, and worse practices" such as "revived and celebrated" pagan worship and "beastly practices of ye mad Bacchanalians." Tensions escalated until Morton declared May Day 1628 the beginning of the "Revels of a New Canaan" and enacted a series of unholy rites and "pagan odes" to Neptune and Triton.

This last blasphemy roused the Puritan colonists to action. The Plymouth militia under Captain Miles Standish attacked Merrymount that June, taking the town and capturing Morton without a single Puritan casualty. After trial, the Puritans marooned him on the deserted Isles of Shoals off New Hampshire, from which he somehow escaped and returned to England. The sober and fearful Plymouth colonists left the remaining Merrymount settlers to their own devices for nearly a year, evidently hoping that the cult would wither and die without its leader. At this time, Puritan records stop referring to the town as Merrymount. By 1629, Morton's settlement had instead become widely known as a "place of woe" called Mount Dagon, after the Canaanite sea god its residents were said to have worshipped.

Throughout Morton's banishment, storms and famine beset the Puritan settlements across the Massachusetts Bay Colony. Starving settlers from Salem under John Endecott raided Mount Dagon once more: they destroyed the May-pole, looted a large quantity of food from a warren of tunnels and subterranean storerooms, and then burned Mount Dagon to the ground. The remaining denizens returned with the raiders to Salem, some eventually moving north to the sheltered harbor that would become Kingsport in 1639, or to a fertile coastal plain at the mouth of the Manuxet River, where along with newly arrived colonists from the south coast of England they founded Innsmouth in 1643. That same year Morton returned from England to his patron Ferdinand Gorges' colony in Maine, settling near Newport Lake (now Sebasticook Lake), the site of a fishing weir and cult complex called Sagon-dagon by the local Algonquians, which dates back to 3000 BC.

John Dee (1527–1608) served as astrologer, cosmographer, and magus to Queen Elizabeth I, poring over Welsh histories and medieval maps of Hyperborea alike to justify her expansionist policies. He likely acquired his copy of Olaus Wormius' Latin *Necronomicon* during a book-buying trip to Flanders in 1562; although he incorporated some of its insights into his *Liber Logaeth* (1583), the English "Dee translation" is more probably the work of his scryer, the forger Edward Kelley (1555–1597). (Osprey Publishing)

Shortly after Morton's return, a fur trader named Richard Billington erected a stone circle outside Plymouth, following instructions from a Wampanoag "wonder-worker" named Misquamacus. Billington "call'd out of the Sky" an NRE named Ossadogowah, apparently with fatal results. After seven mysterious deaths in the woods near Billington's Stones, in 1645 Governor Bradford ordered the militia to tear down this new "Place of Dagon" and arrest Billington, but the trapper and Misquamacus had by then fallen out. Misquamacus led a mixed band of Wampanoags, Nansets, and Nahiggansets that presumably killed Billington and buried him under a mound of his own stones, still visible 50 years later.

Witch Trials

According to contemporary records, "reports of the Idle" located Billington in "divers places," often as a precursor to witchcraft panic. In 1692, Billington appeared in the woods outside Salem, an area already on edge after the December 1690 lynching of an elderly spinster named Abigail Prinn (née Curwen) for "conversation with a dyvil, formed of living shadow, and of prodigious size." The phantom "dark man" and rumors of Abigail Prinn's curse on Salem sparked an explosion of accusations, trials and executions in Essex County throughout 1692 and 1693.

Abigail Prinn may have been one of the most powerful witches, but her aged sister-in-law, the widow Keziah Mason of Arkham, had supposedly been the most learned. The elusive Mason was one of the last of the Essex County witches to be formally accused (though she was one of the first suspected), and unlike many others the confession of heresy she gave was apparently sincere and uncoerced. Only days into her incarceration while awaiting execution, Keziah Mason vanished from Salem Gaol.

Although the vast majority of the witchcraft allegations were disingenuous or at least mistaken, some reflect a genuine occult practice extant throughout the colonies. The Reverend George Burroughs, hanged in 1692, had lived in Maine among the Pennacook, and revived Morton's cult when he returned. One Hepzibah Lawson swore on July 10, 1692, at the Court of Oyer and Terminer under Judge Hathorne, that "fortie Witches and the Blacke Man were wont to meete in the Woodes behind Mr. Hutchinson's house," and one Amity How declared at a session of August 8 before Judge Gedney that "Mr. G. B. [Reverend George Burroughs] on that Nighte putt ye Divell his Marke upon Bridget S., Jonathan A., Simon O., Deliverance W., Joseph C., Susan P., Mehitable C., and Deborah B." Some of the suspected fled before they could be accused, among them the rumored wizards Edward Hutchinson and Edmund Carter, the Bishop and Whateley families who founded Dunwich that year, and Prinn's son Joseph.

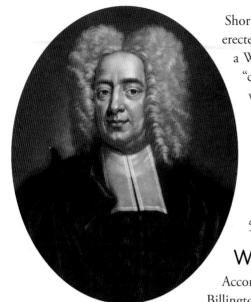

Minister, antiquarian, and scientist Cotton Mather (1663–1728) encouraged and supported the witch-cult purges in Salem and Arkham. He or agents in his circle also investigated the Salem necromancer Simon Orne, the disappearance of Keziah Mason, an unnamable beast-form in Arkham, and the first Ghoul attacks in Boston. Aside from hints he inserted into his *Wonders of the Invisible World* (1693), *Decennium Luctuosum* (1699), and *Magnalia Christi Americana* (1702), we have few records of this first chapter of the Cthulhu War in America. (LOC)

The Case of Joseph Curwen

Joseph Curwen arrived in free-thinking Providence from Salem in June of 1692 and rapidly built a lucrative shipping business and a solid bourgeois identity. However, as rumors spread of his strange practices – "chymical" experimentation late into the night, frequenting of graveyards, importation of cattle and slaves that vanished without being sold, purchase of curious volumes from Amsterdam and the Levant, strange voices and howls heard from his Pawtuxet farmstead – he became almost a recluse. Those who did see him maintained that Curwen never aged, and a 1746 diary entry by one John Merritt confirms that Curwen owned a copy of the *Necronomicon*.

Curwen intended his 1763 marriage to Eliza Tillinghast to provide social cover and a way back into Providence civic life. Instead it provided him a deadly enemy in the person of Eliza's jilted lover Ezra Weeden, who began a jealous surveillance of Curwen's activities. When the British customs schooner *HMS Cygnet* captured the scow *Fortaleza* in January 1770 and discovered a cargo of Egyptian mummies, Weeden used the scandal to interest a vigilance committee of Providence's leading citizens, among them the ex-governor Stephen Hopkins, the astronomer Benjamin West, and the privateer captain Abraham Whipple. The committee intercepted Curwen's mail, uncovering correspondence with one Jedediah Orne of Salem, a William van der Heyl of Chorazin, New York, and an unnamed savant in Philadelphia.

After a year of further surveillance and deliberation, the discovery of a naked man drowned in the creek near Curwen's farm – apparently the blacksmith Daniel Green, who had died almost 50 years earlier in 1721 – moved the committee to action. A detachment of 100 men from the Providence militia under Captain Whipple raided Curwen's Pawtuxet farm and the underlying caverns, firing upon the few men loyal to Curwen at the farm and setting fire to the outbuildings. They used black-powder charges to collapse the tunnels, eventually capturing and killing Curwen himself. As they did, a red mist rose over the farm, blotting out the stars. A contemporary letter describes "an intolerable stench" followed by a "clutching, amorphous fear." Then "came the awful voice which no hapless hearer will ever be able to forget. It thundered out of the sky like a doom, and windows rattled as its echoes died away. It was deep and musical; powerful as a bass organ, but evil as the forbidden books of the Arabs. What it said no man can tell, for it spoke in an unknown tongue."

This is an early (1782?) version of the portrait of Commodore Abraham Whipple (1733–1819) by Edward Savage (1761–1817). Savage sketched Whipple, and apparently heard more details of the captain's later anti-Mythos expeditions, during the siege of Charleston in 1780. Whipple encountered and escaped the creature Savage depicts as a kraken during his 1776 raid on New Providence in the Bahamas. After 1784, Whipple retired inland to a life of farming. (PD)

Captain Esek Hopkins (1718–1802) joined the Curwen raiders at the last minute, commanding the party that closed and explored the tunnels under Pawtuxet. This experience may have deranged him slightly: Congress relieved him of his command in 1778 for disobedience (or excessive initiative) and over his practice of torturing British prisoners to gain information.
(Classic Imag / Alamy)

Governor Hopkins' correspondent Paul Revere led a similar raid on the Orne house in Salem the same night, but their target had decamped the night before. Hopkins had no useful contacts in the distant wilds of upstate New York, but in May 1780, George Washington (possibly alerted by Hopkins) ordered the semi-invalided Lieutenant Colonel Aaron Burr to take a company of men and root out Van der Heyl from Chorazin. Burr and Washington never recorded the results of the action, but during the day of May 19, a profound darkness blanketed the region from Maine to New Jersey. City buildings in Providence could not be seen at noon without the aid of candles. The unnatural darkness lasted more than 24 hours, ending with a rain of sulfurous ash and cinders that fell in some places to a depth of 6in.

The Web-Footed Regiment

Whether because the trials had truly rooted out the witch-cult, or because the witch-cult had learned better security, spiritual threats dominated the colonial imagination less in the mid-18th century. With the threat from France and her Native allies followed by a British crown determined to quash colonial self-government, Patriot elites ignored or even recruited those whom their Puritan forefathers had condemned. By 1759, volunteer regiments from across New England had been raised to press the interests of the British crown in North America, with men from Marblehead, Kingsport, Salem, and Arkham serving with distinction in numerous land campaigns.

(OPPOSITE)

At 10.00pm on April 12, 1771, approximately 100 men of the Providence militia gathered at the Golden Lion Inn on Weybosset Point near Pawtuxet, Rhode Island, and at midnight staged to the nearby Fenner farm. Their leader, the shipping magnate (and future Congressman) John Brown (1736–1803) told the Fenners the militia were moving against a British informant damaging the local smuggling trade: their target was in fact the farm next door, belonging to the necromancer Joseph Curwen. The vigilance committee divided its forces into three: 20 men under the sailor Eleazar Smith to guard the farm's dock against surprise reinforcements, 20 men under Captain Esek Hopkins (1718–1802) to break into and guard a tunnel from the farm to the river valley, and the remaining 60 under Captain Abraham Whipple (1733–1819) to assault the farm itself. Whipple led 20 men against the farmhouse, Captain James Mathewson (1739–80) led 20 against a stone outbuilding, and Brown

commanded the reserve encircling the farm. Whipple, Mathewson, and Hopkins launched their assault shortly after 1.00am. Eight of the raiders died in the affray, as did Curwen and his two servants.

Here, Mathewson's company breaks down the door to the stone outbuilding after Whipple's first whistle blast signals the assault. (A second blast signaled the advance after entry was secured.) Mathewson holds a cutlass and pistol; the man holding the book is the Baptist Reverend James Manning (1738–1791), first president of Brown University. According to the diary of Eleazar Smith, Manning accompanied Mathewson's detachment and emerged "badly disturbed." Surviving correspondence from the Fenner family mentions the "shaft of green light" that emerged from the stone building during Curwen's operations and shone with particular lividity on the night of the attack.

Colonel John Glover's famous 14th Continental "Amphibian" Regiment, officially based out of Marblehead, was made up of just these sorts of men: fishermen, traders, free African-Americans, Wampanoag and other Natives, and Miskatonic Valley farmers. Glover's "web-foots" were instrumental in securing the evacuation of the untested Continental Army – and George Washington himself – from Long Island in July 1776 to avoid a British siege, silently ferrying men, horses, equipment, and supplies across the East River. Particularly wide-eyed accounts of the evacuation credit the sudden thick fog that provided cover for the Continental escape to the strange shanties manned by a few "frog-eyed men of Innsmouth," or in one case to an "artifice" by Colonel Israel Hutchinson of Salem, commander of the 27th Massachusetts. Glover and Hutchinson's regiments also crewed the boats in which Washington crossed the Delaware during the Trenton–Princeton campaign, but the Innsmouth and Kingsport men mostly mustered out in early 1777, disliking the prejudicial attitudes of the regular soldiers.

One Kingsport veteran of Glover's regiment, Richard Holt, served in the Barbary Wars. Captured aboard the *USS Philadelphia* by "Moorish witchcrafts," he spent the bulk of his captivity enslaved to one of the Pasha's pet sorcerers. Upon his release in 1805, Holt returned to Kingsport and built a house on Water Street near the sea. Holt reappears in the correspondence of Glover's political patron Elbridge Gerry in 1813 and 1814; Vice-President Gerry repeatedly and inexplicably attempted to once more recruit the 60-year-old Holt into the US Navy. He was apparently unsuccessful, although he penned an effusive letter of thanks to Holt on August 26, 1814, the day after a sudden hurricane and tornado drove British forces out of Washington.

THREAT REPORT: GHOULS

"There was vaguely anthropoid structure, all right; and the blood corpuscles were almost human – quite shockingly so. But the head and the spade-like appendages and the muscular developments were quite unlike any beast or man on this earth."

–Inspector Gordon Craig, Special Subway
Detail, New York Police Department

For all their horrifying habits and strange abilities, the creatures colloquially known as Ghouls are perhaps the least alien of the catalogued and recognized NREs, and perhaps also the youngest. There is no archaeological (or paleontological) evidence of Ghoul populations until well into the Holocene, though their general absence from the fossil record cannot be taken as conclusive: these voracious creatures consume their own dead. The beasts leave no buildings or monuments, and while intelligent enough to read and write, they have no written records (nor indeed, any written language) of their own.

Ghouls do have a globally shared spoken language, primarily made up of gibbers, meeps, and howls. Those whose habitats abut human settlements have proven capable of learning – and speaking – the human languages of the regions they inhabit. Despite the relative lack of advanced cultural structures, Ghoul social groups share remarkably consistent religious structures, almost universally revering a nameless "charnel god" which, based on limited observation of Ghoul religious rites, is likely the echo of (or the origin for) the child sacrifice-demanding Canaanite-Punic god Moloch.

Roughly equivalent to humans in size, shape, and proportion, Ghouls are facultative bipeds – able to walk or run on four limbs as easily as two. They have small noses set back on a dog-like snout filled with sharp, rending teeth. Most have gray or greenish skin, long, clawed fingers on thick, spade-shaped hands uniquely suited to rapid digging or burrowing, and muscular legs ending in long feet with bony outgrowths that in some cases resemble hooves. Muscle tissue is thin and ropelike but unusually dense, giving the creatures greater strength and stamina than a human of similar size. Ghouls are mortal but long-lived, typically living well into their second century, but can be killed by gunfire of sufficient volume and caliber.

The prevailing theory among MAJIC xenobiologists is that Ghouls are, in fact, a symbiosis between a human being and an aggressive, viral (or prion-based) infection. Following extended or frequent contact with Ghouls, particularly in their own warrens, humans manifest Ghoul traits (both physical and neurological) and, with continued exposure, can completely metamorphose into the Ghoul state. In rare cases, humans and Ghouls have produced viable offspring, although the extant legendry surrounding them more often describes human cults trading "changeling" children with Ghouls.

Ghouls live and travel in packs ranging in size from eight to approximately 60, with multiple packs sometimes gathering to form larger (and often temporary) cooperative social groups near particularly plentiful food sources. Carrion eaters that almost always prefer to feed on human flesh, Ghouls have been observed hunting live prey in rare cases. Long-settled cities with plentiful supplies of human dead have the largest Ghoul warrens in the United States: elaborate networks of caves and tunnels, sometimes dug into solid rock, typically leading to and from graveyards or catacombs. Major warrens exist beneath Boston, New York, Philadelphia, St. Louis, and Detroit. No census or even estimate of the Ghoul population in the United States exists.

Worse yet, Ghouls can traverse stable wormholes between the physical universe as we understand it and a harmonically resonant quantum pocket universe referred to in MAJIC documents as the "Dreamlands." It is unclear if Ghoul biology somehow enables this ability, or if it is instead a hypergeometric or hyperspatial characteristic of the Ghoul tunnels themselves. Regardless, it allows Ghouls effectively unfettered access to virtually any otherwise secure facility on Earth. Shoot-on-sight rules of engagement are thus in place.

A LONELY AND CURIOUS COUNTRY (1804–1927)

"And now, friends and countrymen, if the wise and learned philosophers of the elder world, the first observers of mutation and aberration, the discoverers of maddening ether and invisible planets, the inventors of Congreve rockets and Shrapnel shells, should find their hearts disposed to inquire, what has America done for the benefit of mankind?"

—President John Quincy Adams

Before European contact, the North American continent possessed a number of civilizations approaching or surpassing those of classical antiquity in social sophistication and cultural organization. By the second millennium CE, Cahokia on the Mississippi, the Mound Builders in the Ohio valley and Southeast, and the Anasazi in the Southwest had all created vast trade networks

This 19th-century engraving purportedly depicts Panfilo de Zamacona y Nuñez (1512–1545?) hunting Indians in Mexico with dogs, an ironic reference to Zamacona's description of the K'n-Yani hunting and devouring the devolved semi-human "gyaa-yothn." Although such atrocities were hardly uncommon among conquistadors such as Pedro de Ávila (1468–1531) there is no evidence of Zamacona having done so. (LOC)

and burgeoning towns – only the Northeast coast and Great Plains remained pastoral, possibly due to ongoing Deep One and Mi-Gö depredations, or incursions from the subterranean alien kingdoms of K'n-Yan. The Mandan legend of the Awigaxa band that vanished for three years, after which a remnant returned "talking differently," may be a record of such a conflict.

Then in the 14th century, even before the plagues and invasions associated with European conquest, everything fell apart. Cahokia's citizens completely abandoned their city by 1400. The Buzzard Cult spread nihilist chaos through the mound country, leaving only the Yig-worshippers in Ohio and the solar dictatorship of the Natchez behind. In the west, the Anasazi succumbed to cannibalism or Ghoul attacks.

Without the technological base to ride out these shocks, the population density north of the Rio Grande plummeted, as it had several times before. The smallpox epidemics that followed European contact further devastated Native American societies, which had no natural resistance to the disease. Desperate shamans turned to the worship of more dangerous spirits, invoking the Old Ones and usually suffering the inevitable consequences. Whole nations simply disintegrated or vanished. When American explorers entered the West, they entered a quite literally post-apocalyptic landscape.

Opening the Frontier

By August 1804, US Army Captain Meriwether Lewis and 2nd Lieutenant William Clark had made camp on the north bank of the Missouri River near present-day Vermillion, South Dakota, and had just concluded negotiations with chieftains of the Lakota Sioux nation to allow them to approach an ancient mound believed by several of the surrounding tribes to be cursed. The so-called Spirit Mound, in particular, had come to Lewis and Clark's attention because of the potential military threat it represented. According to Clark, the mound was supposed:

> "... to be the residence of Deavels. That they are in human form with remarkable large heads ... that they are very watchful and are arm'd with Sharp arrows with which they Can Kill at a great distance; they are Said to kill all persons who are So hardy as to attempt to approach the hill; they state that tradition informs them that many Indians have Suffered by these small people. So much do the Maha [Omaha], Soues [Sioux], Ottoes [Otoes] and other neighboring nations believe this fable, that no Consideration is Sufficient to induce them to approach the hill. One evidence which the Inds give for believing this place to be the residence of some unusual Spirits is that they frequently discover a large assemblage of Birds about this mound ...."

Lewis and Clark both remarked in their journals only that the mound offered a clear view of the surrounding territory. They had left St. Louis some three

months before on a mission to explore and map the nearly 830,000 square miles of the Louisiana Territory, and their examination of the Spirit Mound "greatly assisted" their surveys. Although neither man mentions any overt supernatural occurrence, Lewis's original journals were lost following his mysterious death on the Natchez Trace in 1809, and Clark's show signs of re-copying. Sergeant Charles Floyd, one of the 12 men who accompanied Lewis and Clark to the devil-haunted mound, died of a mysterious affliction only hours after the party returned.

The Kingdom Below

Lewis and Clark had in fact found a disused northern outpost of the vast underground kingdom of K'n-Yan, a once-advanced but decadent alien civilization first discovered by the Spanish conquistador Panfilo de Zamacona y Nuñez during Coronado's 1541 expeditions into the North American interior to find the fabled Seven Cities of Gold. In an account discovered in 1928, Zamacona described "Xinian" and its capital, Tsath, accessible through the Alabaster Caverns complex of modern-day Oklahoma. According to Zamacona's account, the inhabitants of K'n-Yan were pale humanoids who believed themselves a race separate from mankind. They demonstrated at least limited telepathy and psychometry, and were reportedly able to dematerialize at will. Zamacona, a man of his time, identified them as demons; MAJIC believes them to be an evolutionary offshoot of the pre-human race *Gigantopithecus lemuriensis*, stunted by generations spent underground.

The decadent and isolationist K'n-Yani remained largely aloof from American affairs, though fears that they would ally with Native American tribes above Tsath to acquire fresh slave-stock drove frontier authorities to occasional action. When a Wichita warrior named Gray Eagle brought reports

THE SORTIE OF JOHN WARREN

During the Second Seminole War in 1837, scouts of the 1st Florida Mounted Militia under Colonel John Warren stumbled upon a previously unmapped necropolis of pre-Columbian construction on the outskirts of the Big Cypress Swamp in southern Florida while engaged in an extensive manhunt for the Seminole chief Yaholooche ("Cloud"). Discovering an extensive network of dry tunnels leading deep below the water table near the center of the graveyard, Warren ordered his men to descend into the passages to search for Yaholooche, who he believed was using them to move raiders throughout the region unseen. Warren emerged from the swamp some eight days later, accompanied by only three of his men. US Army records of Warren's service and court-martial were lost during the Civil War, but Warren's grandson Harley provided family copies of the records to the Miskatonic University library in his will after his own unexpected (and unexplained) death in Florida in 1919.

of just such an alliance with the Osage to William Clark, by then Missouri Territory governor, his prior experiences had left him highly sensitive to the threat they represented. Clark reportedly dismissed Gray Eagle's initial reports, but authorized an attack after Gray Eagle presented him with K'n-Yani artifacts and jewelry he claimed to have taken from an Osage brave. Clark encouraged the Osage's neighbors, the Cherokee, to remove the threat. Under Cherokee chief Spring Frog, a hastily assembled band of 500 Cherokee, Choctaw, Chickasaw, and white settlers attacked the Osage settlement of Pasuga near Claremore Mound in October 1817. The Cherokee massacred the Osage while Clark's picked men collapsed the entrance to K'n-Yan in the mound; K'n-Yan did not retaliate.

An Occurrence at Chickamauga

"'We bury our dead,' said a gunner, grimly, though doubtless all were afterward dug out, for some were partly alive."

–Ambrose Bierce, "A Little of Chickamauga"

From a Cherokee word meaning "river of death," Chickamauga Creek had been the site of numerous NRE incursions and encounters, earning it a reputation among the Native tribes of the area as a place to be avoided at all costs. By the second day of the bloody battle waged there in September 1863, dead and wounded on both sides numbered in the thousands, drawing Ghouls from their forgotten warrens or perhaps from the Dreamlands. The battle lines shifted throughout the skirmish. At dusk on September 19, Confederate forces pushed Union troops from the 9th and 35th Indiana Volunteer regiments back into thick woods east of Lafayette Road, forcing them to retreat over their own dead. As they did so, they stumbled on an entire pack of Ghouls already feeding. The terrified soldiers immediately opened fire, prompting the Ghouls to retaliate.

Shortly after dreaming of an immense, empty city Ambrose Bierce (1842–1914?) left home to work at a newspaper, to which trade he returned after his military service during the Civil War. He eventually named the city Carcosa in his fiction, and may have returned there in 1913. In his last letter (to the daughter of this portrait's painter) before his disappearance, he wrote: "As to me, I leave here tomorrow for an unknown destination." (LOC)

In 1837, Colonel John Warren discovered a necropolis hidden in Big Cypress Swamp, pictured here. He may have been drawn there by something found in an immense dry cave (now Warren's Cave) that he also discovered near Gainesville after the Battle of San Belasco Hammock on September 18, 1836. (PD)

Ambrose Bierce, a 19-year-old lieutenant commanding a company of the 9th Indiana, ordered a retreat as quickly as possible, leaving the men of the 35th and the pursuing Confederates to fight off the enraged and hungry Ghouls. Bierce was part of an old family of witch-hunters and occultists that traced its lineage to William Bradford, the Puritan governor who had orchestrated the downfall of the Dagon cult at Merrymount in 1626. An infantryman from his unit later wrote that Bierce, regarded as standoffish by his men, had drawn "some sign in the yellow dust of the road when he saw them coming," calling down "the attentions of some devil or angel to push back the screaming things."

The 35th Indiana's Company B found itself in the center of the action, losing almost half its fighting strength. The men lost to the Ghouls were listed as missing by both sides, with the surviving officers barely able to provide a coherent report of the action. Although Bierce had correctly assessed the threat and had successfully withdrawn his unit, he bitterly regretted abandoning the 35th to the monsters, as well as the supernatural attention he had drawn to himself to assure his own escape. Years later, Bierce wrote, "when I ask myself what has happened to Ambrose Bierce the youth, who fought at Chickamauga, I am bound to answer that he is dead." Bierce disappeared in Mexico in 1913.

Other Ghoul Skirmishes

Chickamauga was the first significant engagement between American soldiers and Ghouls, but it would not be the last. Though they had coexisted with humans in relative peace for thousands of years, three factors drew Ghouls into human territory and forced men into uncharted realms that had once been the Ghouls' alone: the skyrocketing human population; mass deaths from epidemics (especially the great influenza of 1918–20) and warfare; and aggressive infrastructure development to support an increasingly industrialized America.

The New York Subway

Beginning as early as 1899, the engineers building subway tunnels beneath New York City had begun to encroach on the city's Ghoul warren, prompting irregular attacks from the creatures as they lost more and more territory to the roaring trains. By 1916, the Ghouls had massacred at least one trainload of passengers in a deep tunnel between the Battery and 120th Street. Later that year, the NYPD organized a Special Subway Detail to patrol the lower tunnels and drive the Ghouls back. Funded directly from the Mayor's office by a separate dispensation until at least 1939, the Detail received significantly higher pay than regular-duty units, and suffered significantly higher casualties, including the loss of one of its most decorated commanders to friendly fire in 1922.

No Man's Land

Throughout the battlefields of World War I, tunnels and trenches intruded on Ghoul warrens, and those that did not soon found hungry Ghouls tunneling into No Man's Land to meet them. Repeated exposure to the carrion-eating creatures drew some men to join them; several may have become ghouls themselves. In his 1920 memoir *The Squadroon*, a particularly perceptive British officer named Lieutenant Colonel Ardern Arthur Hulme Beaman wrote that by 1918 the abandoned trenches and No Man's Lands in northern France were "peopled with wild men … deserters, who lived there underground, like ghouls among the mouldering dead. [They] came out at night to plunder and to kill … [we] often heard inhuman cries and rifle shots coming from that awful wilderness as though the bestial denizens were fighting among themselves."

Tempest Mountain

New York Sun reporter Arthur Munroe disappeared in April 1921 near Lefferts Corners, a rural community in the Catskills. Subsequent investigations led the state police to request temporary support from the NYPD's Special Subway Detail, who quickly located the remains of at least four men, including Munroe, and ordered the Martense mansion on Tempest Mountain demolished. Several nearby hills were also blasted in an effort to collapse a network of tunnels burrowed into the rocky ground below the abandoned estate. The Department of Comparative Anatomy at Miskatonic University acquired the Ghoul remains found in the rubble; Dr Francis Morgan's resulting papers remain among the only publicly available studies of Ghoul physiology, and may have inspired the last avant-garde works of Boston artist Richard Upton Pickman.

Some Civil War commanders developed an almost preternatural sense for Ghoul depredations nearby. According to rumor, Colonel Albert Delapore (1819–66) of the Virginia cavalry (shown here in the casual half-uniform common to Virginia militia officers) even used Ghouls to cut off Union patrols or reinforce his own attacks. Union cavalry burned his plantation at Carfax in the Shenandoah Valley as retribution for his "inhuman methods of war," and he died shortly after the war's end, possibly killed by his former slaves avenging previous nameless brutalities. (Osprey Publishing)

In this photograph of Wichita cavalry scouts serving with the Union forces during the Civil War, Gray Eagle is the second from the right. Although Wichita tradition holds that the Gray Eagle who instigated the 1817 attack on Pasuga is the same Gray Eagle who lived at the Wichita station near the Hydro mound in Oklahoma in 1928, it's more likely that they were identically named members of the same family of shamans. (LOC)

This photograph of magician Harry Houdini (1874–1926) and President Theodore Roosevelt (1858–1919) was taken in 1914, shortly after Roosevelt's return from his secret (and nearly disastrous) expedition into the Brazilian interior. Houdini had done covert work for the US Secret Service as early as 1899, and worked for Roosevelt in Russia in 1903 (and possibly in Egypt in 1910). He also collaborated closely with H. P. Lovecraft, planning a major joint investigation into the witch-cult before his sudden and mysterious death on Halloween 1926. (LOC)

The R'lyeh Upheaval

Whether because of the rise in cult activity, the dramatic increase in Pacific naval traffic, or both, the sunken city of R'lyeh experienced a paroxysm of tectonic upheavals in 1889, throwing half-billion-year-old border outposts of the star-spawned empire back above the waves. This seismic calamity and its aftershocks caused several earthquakes, volcanic eruptions, and tsunamis

around the Pacific Plate that year, including disasters at Kumamato, Suwanosejima, Manam, and Banua Wuhu. Storms and psychic disturbances also hammered the Pacific Rim following the upheaval, perhaps most notably at Apia harbor on the Samoan island of Tutuila, relatively close to the epicenter of the R'lyeh event.

Competing for influence in the Pacific Islands, the United States and Germany had both sent small flotillas to Tutuila to protect their respective commercial interests on the island. Both sides were engaged in a tense standoff inside the harbor on March 13, observed by a single British vessel, when the atmospheric pressure suddenly dropped and the native Samoans began fleeing the port. Despite the fact that the crews on both sides were filled with experienced Pacific sailors, the psychic backlash stunned both sides: neither American nor German sailors were able to secure their vessels for the coming storm or to evacuate the harbor. When a cyclone smashed into the island, it severely damaged vessels on both sides, sinking two German ships and leaving the American craft beached or caught on reefs near the harbor.

The psychic echoes of the 1889 event spurred smaller or dormant cults to greater activity. By 1905, an informal student fraternity at the Rhode Island School of Design had begun using NRE imagery in its initiation rites. The wizard Noah Whateley bred his daughter Lavinia to Yog-Sothoth in 1912; Innsmouth sorceress Asenath Waite conspired with Aleister Crowley during his American sojourn in 1919. The Bohemian Club in San Francisco purchased an isolated redwood grove in 1899 at the prompting of member Ambrose Bierce; they erected a stone idol in the shape of an owl there in 1929. In Brooklyn, the occultist Robert Suydam attempted his magical resurrection in 1925 through a resurgent cult of the owl-goddess Mormo, although the February 28, 1925 aftershock of the 1889 event may have triggered him.

Professor of Semitic Languages at Brown University, George Gammell Angell (1857–1926) is shown here with part of his collection of glass bottles, begun during his Tulane University lecturing residency in 1910–11. Professor Angell was the first scholar to assemble evidence of a worldwide Cthulhu cult; his death in December 1926 may well have been no accident. (LOC)

Perhaps most notably, isolated fishermen and voodoo practitioners in the bayous and swamps of Louisiana began organizing ecstatic black masses and animal sacrifices in formal worship of Cthulhu. It was not until the bayou cult began offering up human sacrifices, however, that any of this activity received sustained official attention.

The St. Bernard Parish "Voodoo" Raid

In September 1907, a joint task force formed by the Louisiana State Police and the New Orleans police department traced a woman who had gone missing from a New Orleans slum to nearby St. Bernard Parish, where local law enforcement was already investigating several disturbing reports about the activities of a voodoo cult operating in the swamps. On November 1, a raid led by New Orleans police lieutenant John Raymond Legrasse interrupted one of the cult's ceremonies: the vivisection of a human victim on an altar topped by a statuette depicting Cthulhu himself. Police fired upon the cultists upon discovering the grisly scene, killing five and arresting 47 of an estimated 100 who had been at the ceremony. The rest escaped into the bayou.

Legrasse ordered the excavation of the ceremonial grounds, revealing more than a dozen previous victims, only four of whom were the subject of open investigations. The cultists denied their role in the murders, blaming

Confederate Brigadier General Bushrod Johnson's advance across the Lafayette Road on the afternoon of September 19, 1863, left many scattered Union companies isolated in the woods as night fell. That first day of the Battle of Chickamauga produced over ten thousand fresh corpses, an irresistible banquet for the local Ghoul population, and for the bands of Ghouls following the armies. It is impossible to estimate what portion of the 6,000 "missing or captured" at Chickamauga were actually devoured, and how many supposed artillery or saber casualties actually suffered those mutilations from inhuman claws and incisors.

The "night fight at Chappell's Farm" is usually ignored in official histories of the battle. The surviving remnant of Sergeant Thomas Kennedy's platoon (Company B, 35th Indiana) managed to find a farmhouse to use as a bivouac. Kennedy's diary, recovered by a Confederate intelligence officer from the empty house on the 21st, calls it "Chappell's Farm," but it actually belonged to a schoolteacher named Nobey or Knowby. The Ghoul attack came just after midnight while the men were keeping themselves awake reading a journal they had found in the house. Kennedy wields a saber while Corporal Patrick Molloy (officially listed as a deserter, but mentioned by name in Kennedy's diary) levels a rifle. The Ghouls feed during combat, as Kennedy says: "they [the Ghouls] seem more inclined to dine than fight, as would we in faith likewise be, had we provisions." The last page of Kennedy's diary describes the Union men successfully driving the Ghouls away. A final Ghoul attack likely finished off Kennedy and the other five missing men, although that must remain conjecture. The sole survivor of the action, Private Peter Mulvaney, was captured and sent to Andersonville Prison. He died in the *Sultana* disaster in 1865, and never gave his account of the Night Fight.

"black-winged ones." One cultist, known as "Old Castro," described the cult's faith to interviewers during questioning. The rest focused their evangelism on their fellow prisoners in the St. Bernard lockup. Indeed, one police sergeant would later note:

> *"The men we had in custody could not have cared less about the charges brought against them. In fact, they seemed almost happy to be in jail, where they could try to convert others to their heathen religion. We had to isolate them within the first few hours to stop them from getting whole cell blocks chanting that 'clue clue' nonsense, and to be honest we got real worried that if they spent any time at Angola the whole plantation would be caught up in it! So I guess I'm not too surprised that so many of those old boys died in accidents awaiting trial, or killed themselves, or got caught up with other inmates. No, I'd say it was probably for the best and whoever done it done a public service."*

Records of the suspects' testimony and studies of the few artifacts found in and around the St. Bernard site would form the bedrock of the government's awareness and understanding of the Mythos threat for the rest of the 20th century. Legrasse, and other investigators outside Louisiana, traced the larger cult's connections and even managed some arrests and other disruptions, but the most significant blow would not fall until 20 years later.

THREAT REPORT: DEEP ONES

"No use balking, for there were millions of them down there. They'd rather not start rising and wiping out humankind, but if they were given away and forced to, they could do a lot toward just that... It's not what the fish devils have done, but what they're going to do! They're bringing things up out of where they come from into the town; they've been doing it for years... The houses north of the river between Water and Main streets is full of them, the devils and what they have brought, and when they get ready ... ever hear of a shoggoth?"

–Zadok Allen of Innsmouth, as reported by informant Robert M. Olmstead

Analysis of satellite imagery and Cold War-era sonar surveys suggest that there are no fewer than 28 substantial Deep One colonies across the globe, each with an estimated population of over a million, to say nothing of their hundreds of coastal outposts. They have also colonized human myths: as *Rusalki* in Slavic lore, *Adaro* on the Solomon Islands, *Jiaoren* in South China, *Heqet* to the ancient Egyptians and *Kulullû* in Babylon. Even in the Saharan kingdom of Mali, a thousand miles inland, they appear as the *Nommo*. They have even founded human dynasties: the ichthyoid *Oannes* founded Eridu in southern Mesopotamia, and the earliest Merovingian kings of France were said to descend from a five-horned aquatic *Quinotaur*.

MAJIC paleontologists posit that *Triadobatrachus sapiens* appeared approximately 15 million years ago during the Miocene Epoch, and interbred with hominids from that point on. But they could be even older. Captured specimens, some in US government custody since 1928, have demonstrated the ability to survive without food for decades, and broad immunity to diseases and toxins. Mature adults do not age, but grow throughout their lifetimes to an unknown maximum size: Navy personnel filmed two specimens larger than *Los Angeles*-class submarines in the South Pacific in 1974 during Project *Azorian*. Deep Ones can be killed, but anything short of a fatal wound heals quickly.

In populations isolated from coastal waters, Deep Ones form mated pairs and typically produce single live young which gestate for 10 to 12 months before birth. In rarer (but far from unknown) cases, Deep One communities near human population centers seek human mates (typically pairing male humans with female Deep Ones), breeding hybrids that appear entirely human at birth.

Deep One hybrids are raised on land, reaching an initial physical maturity after puberty just as true humans do before undergoing a second maturation – possibly due to a mitochondrial retrovirus unique to the Deep Ones' genetic heritage – typically beginning between ages 38 and 51.

During this second transformation, usually occurring over a period of five to seven years, ears shrink, eyes bulge, and the skull plates shift to create a narrow crest. Skin becomes rough and then begins to slough off as the hybrid develops scales in the lower dermal layers, until the hybrid takes on the full suite of Deep One traits. Isolated attempts to slow or reverse the transformations have been unsuccessful; unless prevented, a fully mature hybrid will slip into the sea to join its "family" once the physiological alterations are complete. Although human hybrids are by far the most numerous (and the most immediately threatening to US security interests), scattered reports suggest that Deep Ones have also developed similar hybrid breeding relationships with marine mammals such as dolphins.

The precise numbers of these hybrids – pre- or post-transformation – remain unknown, as Deep One traits breed true for up to four generations beyond initial contact: great-great-grandchildren may carry Deep One traits, and their mysterious agendas, without any knowledge of what they must one day become. Consequently, Deep One hybrids represent an almost perfect "fifth column." Efforts to develop medical screening or even genetic sequencing protocols to weed out Deep One hybrids before their second transformation have thus far proven fruitless. Indeed, the possibility cannot be discounted that they have already extensively penetrated critical institutions, including MAJIC.

INNSMOUTH
AND AFTER (1928–45)

"During the winter of 1927–28 officials of the Federal government made a strange and secret investigation of certain conditions in the ancient Massachusetts seaport of Innsmouth. The public first learned of it in February, when a vast series of raids and arrests occurred, followed by the deliberate burning and dynamiting – under suitable precautions – of an enormous number of crumbling, worm-eaten, and supposedly empty houses along the abandoned waterfront. Uninquiring souls let this occurrence pass as one of the major clashes in a spasmodic war on liquor.

Keener news-followers, however, wondered at the prodigious number of arrests, the abnormally large force of men used in making them, and the secrecy surrounding the disposal of the prisoners. No trials, or even definite charges were reported; nor were any of the captives seen thereafter in the regular gaols of the nation. There were vague statements about disease and concentration camps, and later about dispersal in various naval and military prisons, but nothing positive ever developed. Innsmouth itself was left almost depopulated, and it is even now only beginning to show signs of a sluggishly revived existence."

–H. P. Lovecraft, "The Shadow Over Innsmouth"

This photograph of Abigail Waite (1853–1928?) taken *c.*1890 depicts a typical case of the "Innsmouth Look" in Deep One-human hybrids. (Propnomicon)

When the St. Bernard Parish investigations revealed the sinister implications of the growth of a nationwide Cthulhu cult to Louisiana authorities, there was no single agency able or empowered to assess the rising threat posed by hidden pre-human populations and prehistoric doomsday cults. It is probably a coincidence that, only seven months after Legrasse's raid, President Theodore Roosevelt ordered the Justice Department to create a national Bureau of Investigations (the direct forerunner of the FBI) over Congressional objections. On the other hand, Roosevelt was a devoted collector of Western legendry and a former New York City police commissioner: he might well have

come across legends of K'n-Yan (Gray Eagle is reported to have survived well into the 20th century), or evidence of Ghoul attacks, or both.

Lousiana State Police forwarded their files on the St. Bernard Parish raid to the Bureau of Investigations in 1909, Bureau Chief Stanley Finch had the files classified and compartmented in a special unit he christened Unit 10, sometimes referred to in contemporary documents as "Unit X." Finch charged Unit 10 first with gathering information on state and local investigations into NRE-related activity, and then with mounting its own inquiries. Unit 10 assisted in several raids over the next two decades, often under cover of, or cooperating with, anti-sedition or anti-terrorism actions against Communists or anarchists, which many nihilist NRE cultists were. Another common cover was Prohibition enforcement against bootleggers and moonshiners, as with the Robert Suydam case at Red Hook in 1925. With almost 15 years' experience behind it when the Innsmouth cult revealed itself, the Bureau thought it was ready.

The decrepit state of Innsmouth even before the 1928 Raid can be seen in this photograph of the Eliot Street Pier, taken in 1925 by Michael Schefter, a factory inspector with the Massachusetts Department of Public Safety. (Propnomicon)

Casus Belli

The ongoing effects of the 1837 depression left most of the businesses in Innsmouth under the control – direct or otherwise – of shipping magnate Obed Marsh, who leveraged his profitable Pacific trade into ownership of the town's mills and even a gold refinery. His success attracted followers, whom he initiated into a Tahitian cult disguised as a fraternal organization called the Esoteric Order of Dagon. Enemies of the cult disappeared or drowned

The basalt Nan Madol complex on the Caroline island of Ponape served as the capital of a Cthulhu cult from approximately 1100 to 1628, when the local workers overthrew the Chau-te-leur dynasty, a clear cognate name to the NRE. *Nan Madol* means "the spaces between," a clear reference to alien hyperspace (as the *Necronomicon* says: "Not in the spaces we know, but between them, They walk serene and primal") and furthermore, the complex rests on the *Soun Nan-Leng* reef. ONI feared that the German, then the Japanese, occupiers of Ponape would restore the cult and contact the Deep One city of Kahnihmw off the shore of the Nan Madol lagoon. (robertharding / Alamy)

until 1846, when a citizens' vigilance committee led by Selectman Herman Mowry arrested Marsh and his acolytes. Two weeks later, half the population of the town (including Selectman Mowry) was dead and Marsh returned to power. Outsiders were told a plague had ravaged the town, and aside from an increasingly sinister reputation and medical reports of deformities among residents in the following generations (blamed on the effects of the "Innsmouth Plague") the town slipped into relative obscurity after the Civil War.

Nevertheless, official interest in Innsmouth slowly renewed. In 1917, Draft officials in the town reported impossible deformities, and during World War I the Office of Naval Intelligence (ONI) initiated an internal investigation into several sailors from the Innsmouth area who proved unreliable in action: specific charges included smuggling and illicit fraternization, especially on Pacific stations. When confronted with the possibility of an ONI inquiry into the "Pacific ring" in early November of 1920, the Governor of American Samoa, Warren Terhune, shot himself in the heart rather than cooperate with the investigation.

The Case of Earl Hancock Ellis

The case next came to the attention of an eccentric US Marine Corps strategist, Lieutenant Colonel Earl Hancock "Pete" Ellis, who insisted on following up on the odd events in the Pacific personally. He may have first crossed paths with the cult while stationed in New Orleans in 1914, at which point his alcoholism became chronic. In 1921 Ellis brought his concerns to Assistant Secretary of the Navy Theodore Roosevelt, Jr., who gave him permission

Lieutenant Colonel Ellis also predicted the Japanese attacks that would draw the United States into World War II, authoring a comprehensive study of Japanese war plans in 1921, while attached to the Headquarters Marine Corps staff at Quantico. Entitled *Operation Plan 712: Advanced Base Operation in Micronesia*, Ellis's paper correctly predicted both Japanese and American naval strategy in a war more than 20 years in the future.

Ellis had descended into a deep seclusion while writing *Plan 712* throughout the previous year, and friends complained that his behavior had changed radically. The previously enthusiastic officer became standoffish and expressionless, with one friend and colleague complaining that it was as if "he had forgotten, for a time, how to move the muscles of his face." After publishing the plan, Ellis complained of headaches and hallucinations of strange beings and desert cities. Although Ellis never credited his prophetic strategy to any supernatural insight, his MAJIC dossier, partly inherited from the ONI, speculated that Ellis may have been another target of "… the so-called 'Great Race from Yith' so frequently mentioned in connection with the Peaslee case of 1908–1913."

for an undercover mission to the western Pacific Islands. Ellis submitted an undated letter of resignation to the Marine Corps, and then traveled extensively throughout the Caroline and Marshall islands (including Ponape, New Guinea, and other stops on the Marsh trade routes) investigating the unidentified force or cult that had prompted Terhune's suicide. Ellis's mental stability deteriorated rapidly and he died, supposedly from alcohol poisoning, on the Japanese-occupied island of Koror on May 12, 1923.

The Office of Naval Intelligence sent Chief Pharmacist Lawrence Zembsch to collect Ellis's remains – and his final reports – as soon as they learned of his death. After examining Ellis's findings, Zembsch asked Japanese authorities to have Ellis's remains exhumed and burned, and cabled an abbreviated version of Ellis's terrified observations to the ONI. Zembsch himself then had a nervous breakdown after being "heavily drugged" by an unidentified assailant. Ellis's complete reports disappeared, and the only other man who had seen them – Zembsch – died when a sudden earthquake smashed into Yokohama where he was recovering.

Operation Ashdod

"And when they of Ashdod arose early on the morrow, behold, Dagon was fallen upon his face to the earth before the ark of the Lord. And they took Dagon, and set him in his place again.

And when they arose early on the morrow morning, behold, Dagon was fallen upon his face to the ground before the ark of the Lord; and the head of Dagon and both the palms of his hands were cut off upon the threshold; only the stump of Dagon was left to him.

Therefore neither the priests of Dagon, nor any that come into Dagon's house, tread on the threshold of Dagon in Ashdod unto this day."

—1 Samuel 5: 3–5

A surprisingly well-publicized photograph of the USS *O-9* (*SS-70*) in the Panama Canal Zone, officially dated to February 22, 1928, a week after the Innsmouth Raid she assisted by torpedoing the Deep One arsenal off Devil's Reef. On the morning of June 20, 1941, while cruising with two other subs off the coast of Maine, an unknown force crushed her hull and pulled her under with the loss of all hands. (PD)

Over the next four years, the ONI followed Ellis's leads in desultory fashion, and Unit 10, cooperating with the Coast Guard, expanded its surveillance to cover bootlegging and other smuggling operations run out of Innsmouth by patriarch Barnabas Marsh. On July 16, 1927, a young anthropology student named Robert Olmstead stumbled into the FBI office in Boston raving with breathless tales of bulging-eyed mutants and alien fish-cults. Unit 10 and the ONI both received Olmstead's report and to their credit recognized the need for joint action: the United States needed to deal with a Deep One threat that had already breached its borders.

Between July 1927 and February 1928, military assets were secretly recalled from police actions in Central America and staged in New England to prepare for Operation *Ashdod* (named from a passage in the First Book of Samuel), a full-scale assault on the Innsmouth threat. The objective was not merely to eradicate the Innsmouth cult, but also to recover sufficient intelligence to finally understand the nature of the "Pacific threat" once and for all. The 66th Company of 1st Battalion, 5th Marine Regiment pulled out of Nicaragua and staged at Camp Devens west of Innsmouth in December to prepare for the operation. The *USS O-9* (also known as *SS-70*), an O-class submarine launched in 1918, providentially ordered to New London from the Panama Canal Zone, began loitering off the coast of Massachusetts in January.

Despite the heavy military component, the operation was led, at least nominally, by the FBI. On the night of February 13, 1928, the Bureau passed down instructions for Massachusetts State Police to close all roads leading to and from Innsmouth. Bureau special agents moved into position at the town limits on Massachusetts state highway 1A, where they briefed Marine Corps troops on the full scope of the assault. At the same time, FBI men aboard the Coast Guard cutter *USCGC General Greene*, based out of Boston, briefed its captain and the commander of the *O-9*, Lieutenant J. T. Acree, received orders to sail into Innsmouth harbor to support a Marine operation against "bootleggers," who were expected to receive support from "the seas east of Devil Reef." Although a little mystified by the order, Acree stationed his boat above a deep submarine gorge near the reef.

The Marines encountered little resistance as they moved through the mostly abandoned streets of Innsmouth until they reached Federal Street. Clearing the ramshackle houses along the route they uncovered several slumbering families, all of whom professed their innocence and surrendered immediately. The Marines attempted to move the families out of the combat zone quietly, so they could continue toward the Marshes' expected strongholds around New Church Green near the town center: the location of the Esoteric Order of Dagon and the Marsh, Gilman, and Eliot estates. However, a young girl and her mother, both of old Innsmouth stock, suddenly turned on their caretakers, wresting a Thompson submachine gun from a startled lance corporal and opening fire on the column from the rear.

Taking cover among the residences, the Marines returned fire, and then continued forward – but they knew that the element of surprise was now lost. The Marines began setting fire to homes and businesses as they passed them to ensure against another unexpected attack, and for the remainder of the battle surrendering townsfolk were shot out of hand, any survivors being taken as prisoners to the staging area outside town. Although this tactic (honed in the Philippines and Nicaragua) almost certainly prevented additional attacks from behind the lines, it also forced the few innocent Innsmouth residents to oppose the Marines, effectively stiffening the town's resistance. Despite the presence of both the *General Greene* and the *O-9* in or near Innsmouth harbor, several belligerents are believed to have escaped into the sea, where they attempted to summon reinforcements from their aquatic cousins in the nearby Deep One settlement, which recovered records and subsequent interrogations would identify as Y'ha-nthlei.

By 4.00am a Marine mortar barrage breached the Marshes' hastily constructed defenses, allowing a platoon of Marines to begin a room-by-room attack on the old Masonic temple that had served the Esoteric Order of Dagon as its headquarters for almost 90 years. For the first time, the Marines found themselves in open battle with Deep One hybrids, and the under-prepared unit began taking heavy casualties.

At about the same time, *O-9* detected the first significant Deep One activity in the gorge just beyond Devil Reef, reporting "flashes of light" and "a low, moaning roar that rattled the hull so hard it popped rivets." Whether they were warned by fleeing hybrids or contacted telepathically, the Deep Ones were stirring. As the submarine dove below increasingly choppy seas, the *O-9*'s hydrophones detected a large object rushing toward the boat from the canyon. Acree ordered the crew to fire torpedoes, ultimately collapsing the walls of the canyon before the creature – if creature it was – could emerge. MAJIC's official assessment later classified the *O-9*'s target as a huge amorphous bioweapon known as a Shoggoth, but given the limited sensor capability of the O-class submarine no definitive determination can be made.

Despite the loss of almost half a platoon in under an hour, the Marines ultimately eliminated the resistance within the Esoteric Order of Dagon's temple, while the rest of the company moved on the massive, labyrinthine homes of Innsmouth's most powerful residents. Even given the warning of machine-gun fire in the early stages of the attack, Innsmouth's inhuman residents had been unable to prepare an adequate defense. By dawn, Operation *Ashdod* was over: the Marines withdrew, taking 249 prisoners back to Camp Devens, and Unit 10 began securing the town's records, family libraries, financial documents, and Deep One artifacts for further study.

The Innsmouth Aftermath

"I am … contagious… I request you not to investigate the conditions of my death."
–Columbia University anthropologist Buell Halvor Quain

On February 14, 1928, the United States government learned it had been at war for longer than it had been in existence. The Innsmouth raid took so many prisoners, and recovered so much intelligence – not just the crumbling tomes and scriptures from the Esoteric Order of Dagon hall, but bills of lading and payment from the Marsh Refinery – that the scope of the "Cthulhu cult" was finally, and terrifyingly, laid bare. An initial survey of captured documents broadly hinted that multiple species of nonhuman intelligences were arrayed against the United States specifically and humanity more generally, effectively threatening a global extinction event if unchallenged. In their first classified after-action report, Unit 10 agents asserted that "we appear to have uncovered a loose organization that transcends boundaries of nation and even species, dedicated to the destruction of this and every other state on earth. The antiquity of some of the documents collected suggests that this goal is long-standing. Their plan, if a strategy that extends across countless generations can even be called that, is already well under way."

Despite the exemplary cooperation between federal criminal investigators and the US Navy throughout Operation *Ashdod*, lines of communication

In 1930, following a prolonged legal battle, the Commonwealth of Massachusetts began to fill the Quabbin Reservoir in the upper Miskatonic and Swift River valleys. The Secretary of War intervened in the case, ostensibly to guard Connecticut's water rights, but in actuality to ensure the drowning of the town of Dunwich, a hotbed of Yog-Sothoth cultism. During the decade the reservoir filled, the Army Air Corps repeatedly bombed Dunwich and other sensitive valley sites including the meteorite-stricken Gardner farmstead: again the War Department cooperated, declaring the future lake bed the Quabbin Reservoir Precision Bombing and Gunnery Range.
(James M. Hunt / Alamy)

began to break down almost immediately afterward. Unit 10 took steps to classify the Innsmouth evidence almost as soon as it was removed from the town. Citing the ONI's open investigation into what now appeared to be a pervasive infiltration of Deep Ones into the Navy's ranks, FBI Director J. Edgar Hoover refused to share either the evidence or the results of the Bureau's analysis with the Navy. This did not prevent the Bureau from turning to private industry to examine its findings – but these first attempts to correlate the contents of the "Innsmouth cache" would end badly.

In early 1930, the Bureau sent several samples of Deep One artifacts and remains to DuPont's Purity Hall laboratory for chemical analysis by the prominent research chemist Wallace Carothers. Although the Purity Hall research did result in several critical breakthroughs – including the development of some of the first practical polyester fabrics – exposure to the alien materials exacerbated Carothers' already serious depression. He committed suicide in a Philadelphia hotel room in April 1937 by drinking a cocktail of cyanide and lemon juice.

Unit 10 read astronomer William Wallace Campbell into its research program in 1935 after he retired from the presidency of the National Academy of Sciences. He was asked to assess the validity of some of the astronomical data found among the Esoteric Order of Dagon's documents, in particular those documents which alluded to alien intelligences in nearby space. Campbell's research was short-lived: by early 1938, he had begun experiencing unexplained neurological disorders that left him blind and unable to speak for long periods at a time. In June of that year, he leapt to his death from a fourth-story window in San Francisco.

The Bureau recruited a young Columbia University anthropologist named Buell Halvor Quain in 1935, following his year-long study of the culture and legends of isolated Pacific islanders. It was thought that Quain's work would leave him well positioned to help translate and analyze certain religious texts and objects taken from the Innsmouth cache. Quain led two expeditions

(OVERLEAF)

The decisive moment of the Innsmouth Raid (on land at least) comes when a squad of Marines led by Lieutenant Allen Schofler advances without orders, entering the Esoteric Order of Dagon temple from Broad Street through a side window rather than supporting the frontal assault across the New Church Green. Caught unprepared, the hierophant (shown in the golden tiara described in Olmstead's testimony but not listed in the official inventory of captured temple paraphernalia) flees through a secret passage into the network of tunnels beneath Innsmouth. Although the two full Deep Ones shown would kill or cripple five men in Schofler's squad before going down in a hail of .45 bullets, the rapid capture of the cult's idol broke the morale of the Marsh clan and their Deep One allies. At the end of the day, the Marines' superior rate of fire and unit cohesion overcame the unnatural stamina of the Innsmouth folk, who were armed (if at all) with spearguns and antique Civil War-era firearms.

A US Marine detachment engages in a reconnaissance in force of Mi-Gö bases in Vermont, following a phosgene gas bombardment by Keystone B-6 bombers. This photograph, taken some time in 1937 or 1938, shows a Marine suffocating after removing his gas mask for unknown reasons: B-8 investigators suggested telepathic control, overwhelming panic, or an unknown side-effect on some personalities from handling Mi-Gö equipment. (Everett Collection Historical/Alamy)

into the Brazilian interior in 1937 and 1938 to locate a native tribe that he believed was still speaking a "pure" (and possibly pre-human) language which underpinned much of the syncretic "Mythos" that the Cthulhu cult had adopted as its own. It was largely through Quain's reports that the term "Mythos" was adopted in government documents after 1937. During his second expedition, Quain came to believe that he had contracted a mysterious linguistic disease; he quarantined himself from all human contact to prevent his condition spreading, finally hanging himself in early August 1939.

While the FBI took the lead in examining, correlating, and cataloguing the Innsmouth cache, the US Navy found itself in charge of almost 250 prisoners, most of whom were only partly human. Initial attempts to hold the prisoners at a single facility were plagued by escape attempts. After having to take extraordinary measures to thwart these attempts throughout the winter and spring of 1928, the ONI had the prisoners separated into small groups and sent to inland military hospitals and prisons throughout the Midwest and Southwest, where their access to so-called "friendly alien populations" was assessed to be less likely.

In the short term, the ONI debriefings were more productive than the Bureau's disastrous attempts to comprehend the scope of their findings. As the Navy began to understand the scope of the threat, it prioritized immediate and aggressive, even ruthless, intelligence gathering. This was not without some cost to its own personnel: one very promising and open-minded investigator, a lieutenant on Pacific station on the *USS Roper,* had to be invalided out when he contracted a pulmonary infection from Deep One secretions. With few exceptions, prisoners whose intelligence value had been exhausted were tried and executed on charges of treason, though a small group of un-indicted detainees were still being held at the State Mental Hospital in Yankton, South Dakota, as late as 1949.

Evolving Defense Schemes

The Navy's rapidly evolving counter-NRE mission was (and would remain) highly compartmented, with ONI officers deployed to several critical locations to monitor the Mythos threat. By 1929, the ONI had secretly tasked a unit in the First Naval District (encompassing most of New England) with monitoring several NRE-linked sites in coastal waters. This watching brief was under the auspices of the district's Communication and Information Service, which until World War I had largely employed local reservists and volunteers. After the Department of the Navy overhauled the entire Naval district system in 1931, this small detachment was renamed Section B-8, and reorganized as a special departmental unit tasked with monitoring current intelligence on potentially Mythos-related activity from all 17 naval districts and re-examining historical holdings to ensure that earlier indications of NRE-related threats had not gone unnoticed.

The discovery of several then-unidentifiable alien corpses – later determined to be Mi-Gö – in the aftermath of the 1936 Northeast Flood led Section B-8 to begin a series of visual surveillance overflights of New England. The overflights allowed B-8 to identify several previously unknown locations in northern Vermont that showed evidence of substantial occupation and excavation, as if the then-unknown creatures were mining the Green Mountains for some unknown but apparently valuable material. Sufficiently concerned about the possibility of additional non-human threats after its Innsmouth experience, the Navy worked quickly to organize three bombing runs over each of the sites, dropping conventional ordnance as well as phosgene and chlorine gas bombs on the sites within weeks of their discovery. The attacks were apparently successful. When a US Marine detachment reached the site on foot, they encountered no resistance, and recovered samples of advanced Mi-Gö technology that had been only slightly damaged in the attacks. In order to ensure that site exploitation could continue without undue public scrutiny, the former Mi-Gö operating base was absorbed by an expansion of the Army's Camp Ethan Allen, which continues to serve as a testing ground for advanced weaponry to this day.

World War II

The outbreak of war in Europe in 1939 served as a significant distraction from the varied threats posed to the United States by Mythos entities; when Japan's attack on Pearl Harbor drew the US into the war in 1941, the immediate

One of the few known photographs of a Unit 10 team in action depicts a squad deploying flamethrowers against part of a small Cthulhu-spawn colony on the island of Eniwetok in February 1944. Unit 10 discovered that Eniwetok rests on a Cretaceous seamount, a major outcropping of Cthulhu's sunken continent of Yhe. Whether the Japanese intended to lure the Americans into a Mythos deathtrap or fortified the atoll in ignorance, the response was overwhelming firepower: the battleships USS *Tennessee* and USS *Iowa*, along with shore artillery, delivered over a kiloton of ordnance against both the Japanese and Mythos threats. (Osprey Publishing)

threat overcame lingering but less pressing concerns about K'n-Yan, Deep Ones, Old Ones, and their supposed alien masters.

One effect of this distraction was that a small Wisconsin publisher brought to press the works of H. P. Lovecraft in three volumes. The ONI did not learn of the leak until 1945, with the publication of *The Dunwich Horror and Other Weird Tales* as #730 in the Armed Services Editions. The dangers posed by the Mythos were not completely forgotten, however: B-8 fell under the auspices of the counter-supernatural Supreme Allied Command: Shadow Theater (SAC:ST), and Vice-President Henry Wallace (an initiate into Central Asian traditions opposed to those of the Mythos) forced Hoover to promise full cooperation with SAC:ST operations, including cross-deployment of liaison personnel.

This hybrid B-8/FBI group, which retained the cryptic designator "Unit 10" throughout the war, tracked a variety of known Mythos actors to ensure non-human elements would not be inadvertently drawn into the war. They hoped that even if NREs and their servitors became formal belligerents, the Allies would not be caught flat-footed. In but one example, Unit 10 maintained

The Château des Fausses Flammes in Auvergne, depicted after its destruction by the Maquis du Mont Mouchet in May 1944. Originally built on a pre-Roman foundation in the 9th or 10th century, Fausses Flammes became the center of a Melusine cult until its destruction by the pious monks of nearby Perigon. The decadent Duc des Esseintes rebuilt the château in 1875 and assembled one of the best occult libraries in Europe there. In 1944, the Nazis' *Projekt Leo* targeted the Fausses Flammes library; a Unit 10 OSS team parachuted in to prevent the books falling into Kaltenbrunner's hands, joining up with the local Resistance for what eventually proved to be a Pyrrhic victory for both. The Germans made off with portions of the library despite the château's destruction; the Maquis were badly mauled in the fight and nearly the entire Unit 10 force ended the operation missing or captured. The confused reports of "living mummies" and "serpent vampires" do little to clear up the mysteries surrounding this obscure engagement. (LOC)

an extensive record of remote Mi-Gö probes penetrating and observing Allied bombing columns, where confused pilots referred to them as "foo fighters." In the Pacific Theater, limited new intelligence and the now-fully analyzed partial reports from Ellis's undercover mission in the Caroline Islands led Unit 10 to issue warnings prompting Allied forces to skip a planned invasion of Ponape during the island-hopping campaign. Instead, dozens of B-24 and B-25 bombers blanketed Ponape despite a limited Japanese presence on the island, and the battleships *USS Iowa* and *USS Massachusetts* bombarded the island on Walpurgisnacht, 1944. Thanks to the Ponape bombardments and an unknown number of other still-classified missions, the worst of Unit 10's fears were never realized.

While Japan grappled with an even more extensive series of Deep One infiltrations in its own Naval ranks, Reichsführer-SS Heinrich Himmler had ensured that Germany devoted significant resources throughout the war to the pursuit of occult knowledge, which he believed held the secret to ensuring Aryan domination over the known world. By the end of 1943, Nazi Germany had amassed the single largest extant cache of Mythos-related tomes, scrolls, and grimoires in existence. SS Obergruppenführer Ernst Kaltenbrunner, the head of the Reichssicherhauptamt (Reich Main Security Office; RSHA), tasked the catalog and study of this Mythos library to a Sicherheitsdienst (Security Service; SD) intelligence officer, SS Obersturmbannführer Werner Göttsch, as part of a program known as *Projekt Leo*. In January 1944, Göttsch consolidated 8,000 occult and Mythos tomes at Burg Niemes in the Sudetenland, where they could be studied "for potential tactical use" as the tide of the war began to shift in the Allies' favor.

Over the following year, Göttsch and his adjutant, Sturmbannführer Hans Richter, collected almost 35,000 books and documents at Burg Niemes. They plundered Masonic libraries, private collections from the Hexenturm at Idstein and the Faussesflammes Chateau in Vichy France, witch-trial archives, and in July even the Abwehr's extensive library. The *Leo* collection included kabalistic texts looted from synagogues, church documents acquired from fascist holdouts in Rome, and (although Allied bombing directed by Unit 10 destroyed the Greek copy at Monte Cassino) a Latin *Necronomicon* recovered from a ruined castle in Romania. Göttsch then selected one hundred of the most significant items and moved them to Altaussee, Austria, where he was to attempt a ceremony to summon a being or force that Kaltenbrunner believed would come to the immediate defense of a Germany under siege. By the time arrangements for the mystical working were complete, however, Allied forces had begun to close in on Austria from both sides. After hearing reports of the brutal Soviet assault on Vienna in April 1945, a terrified Göttsch sent word to nearby American units that he was willing to defect if he could be extracted before Soviet forces arrived, and emphasized that he was willing to hand over whatever he could about *Projekt Leo*.

A Unit 10 team swept into Altaussee to recover Göttsch and his holdings on May 8, 1945, just ahead of a much larger Soviet force. Although Göttsch was extracted successfully, agents were only able to recover less than half of the *Leo* trove before battlefield conditions forced them to retreat. Göttsch spent less than a week in a POW camp in Europe before being transferred to SAC:ST custody. Although his associates were all tried and executed at Nuremberg, Unit 10 recruited Göttsch after a substantial debriefing, and he served the United States in various capacities as an intelligence asset on NRE activity until his disappearance in 1974. There is no evidence that the Soviets captured any *Projekt Leo* personnel after the war, but they had almost certainly secured the remainder of the *Leo* documents for their own use by June 1945.

THREAT REPORT: MEGARKARUA SAPIENS

"Scientists to the last – what had they done that we would not have done in their place? God, what intelligence and persistence! What a facing of the incredible, just as those carven kinsmen and forebears had faced things only a little less incredible! Radiates, vegetables, monstrosities, star spawn – whatever they had been, they were men!"

–Professor William Dyer, "Response to the Report of the 1930–1931 Pabodie Antarctic Expedition"

Megarkarua sapiens, perhaps better known to MAJIC agents as simply "the Elder Things," are believed to have been the first complex multi-cellular organisms on Earth, arriving on the planet from a distant star system approximately 545 million years ago (MYA), just before a sudden explosion of biodiversity among the primitive bacterial life of the Precambrian era. Although some scientists have argued that the timing is mere coincidence, and that animal life would have developed even without the assistance and interference of the Megarkarua, the simple fact remains that many, if not most, of the extant species on this planet arose as the result of their engineering. Consequently, although the Megarkarua are rightly considered aliens by most observers, their place at the origin of what is otherwise considered "native" life on earth suggests that much, if not all, of the observable biodiversity on Earth is of similarly extraterrestrial origin.

Adult *Megarkarua sapiens* stand 2 to 2.7m tall. Their bulging, five-ridged, radially symmetrical bodies are equipped with wings, and thin stalks used for locomotion and grasping protrude from the bottom and center of their bodies. They are incapable of speech but can communicate telepathically with other species. They reproduce by sporification, and in their larval stages appear similar to non-intelligent, native, prehistoric echinoderms: fossilized crinoid Megarkarua young were once thought to be a separate species of echinoderm designated *Arkarua adami*. The creatures can hibernate almost indefinitely in response to isolation or environmental stress, with some living examples known to be at least 80 MYA.

Using bio-engineered alien or terrestrial slave-weapons called shoggoths, the Megarkarua expanded over the entire surface of the Earth, building cities both on land and underwater. The arrival of further extraterrestrial competitors (Flying Polyps ca. 500 MYA; Yithians ca. 450 MYA; Cthulhu ca. 350 MYA) slowly chipped away at Megarkarua dominance, but the real blow to their civilization came from within.

Although not truly sentient, shoggoths are clever, aggressive, and violent. They turned on their masters around 252 MYA, igniting a global war that incidentally drove 85 percent of Earth's species extinct. After a multi-million-year struggle that splintered the continent of Gondwanaland, the Megarkarua defeated the shoggoths, reducing them to a few breeding pits. The inability of shoggoths to breed independently, no doubt a deliberate fail-safe, has since kept them from overwhelming vulnerable native species.

The war crippled the Elder Things, however, leaving them vulnerable to their rivals; the irruption of the Mi-Gö around 130 MYA eventually restricted the Megarkarua to Antarctica and the surrounding continental shelf. The glaciation of Antarctica finally ended the Elder Things' civilization around 15 MYA.

MAJIC considers the few remaining shoggoth breeding pits strategically vital. They serve as a major motivator for the continued US and Russian presence in Antarctica; Russia has maintained a supposedly peaceful scientific base atop an abandoned Megarkarua settlement in Lake Vostok since 1964. Such Megarkaruan ruins can become unstoppable biological weapons factories, but the physical constraints of polar military operations and the dangers of escalating combat with non-dormant shoggoth defenses keep US options limited. The disastrous Pabodie and Starkweather-Moore Antarctic expeditions in the 1930s demonstrated that some Megarkarua have survived their eons-long hibernation; possible Soviet-Megarkarua contacts were an ongoing nightmare for MAJIC planners during the Cold War.

THE COLDEST WAR
(1945–91)

"How can you expect a man who is warm to understand one who is cold?"
–Aleksandr Solzhenitsyn

When President Truman formally disbanded the wartime Office of Strategic Services (OSS) in September 1945, Unit 10 quietly continued operations under the auspices of the War Department's Strategic Services Unit. It was supervised by Curtis V. Ropes, a physics professor who had been drawn into the OSS at OSS Director William Donovan's request in the early days of the war, along with several other New England academics. Despite the vast amount of NRE material uncovered during the war, the Unit 10 operation budget dwindled with the rest of the national security establishment. Uniformed personnel demobilized; academics returned to universities whose student bodies were booming thanks to the GI Bill; and the investigators who had formed the core of the prewar unit were transferred back to the FBI. Hoover considered the Deep One threat contained – and more importantly, he believed in the supremacy of his FBI fiefdom: no outsiders requested or

Pictured receiving the Medal of Merit from President Truman, Secretary of Defense James Forrestal (1892–1949) provided crucial leadership in the postwar creation of MAJIC. He served on its governing committee until Truman fired him in March 1949, at which point he suffered a massive mental breakdown (doubtless caused by exposure to Mythos truths) and entered psychiatric care. On May 22, 1949, corpsmen found Forrestal hanged by the neck from the window of his room at Bethesda Naval Hospital, in circumstances that remain mysterious to this day. (NARA)

required. To defend the nation against the Mythos threat, Dr Ropes relied on a trickle of War Department funding and staff, and on his own powers of persuasion.

A modern view of Thule Air Base in Greenland, established in 1951 near the site of a World War II-vintage USAAF weather station. In 1982, Thule became a USAF Space Command base, monitoring not just ballistic missile launches but Flying Polyp activity in the Van Allen belt and potential alien incursions from extralunar space. (PD)

Pole Positioning

The United States occupied Greenland in 1941 after Denmark fell to Hitler's forces, and postwar strategists intended a permanent military presence to remain on the island. When Ropes found out about the planned deployments, he arranged a special compartmented briefing for Secretary of the Navy James Forrestal, outlining the dizzying array of Mythos dangers in both the north and south polar regions. He urged Forrestal to organize several precautionary expeditions before committing US military personnel to operate in what Ropes believed was effectively enemy territory.

Ropes had reason to be concerned. He had been one of the survivors of the 1930–1931 Pabodie Antarctic Expedition, and after being read into Unit 10 in 1941 had been shocked to learn that then-Commander Richard Byrd's 1928–1929 expedition had actually overflown the same abandoned, prehistoric city where he had left seven of his colleagues dead. On the other side of the world in 1860, Ropes' great-uncle, Princeton anthropologist William Channing Webb, had encountered an isolated Greenland Inuit tribe who practiced a bloodthirsty religion centered around the appeasement of several malevolent demigods who were believed to inhabit the island's glacial interior – and of Cthulhu himself.

THE THULE INCIDENT

MAJIC attempted a tactical nuclear strike against Itlaqqa in January 1968. Most information on the mission remains classified, so it is impossible to determine its success: however, it is known that the B-52G Stratofortress *HOBO 28* crashed onto the sea ice near Thule Air Base on January 22 with only four of its five warheads still on board. A MAJIC tiger team noted in 1998 that following the mission global temperatures began rising after a 30-year plateau; they have now increased by 0.7°C, leading to increased Greenland ice melt. Is this Itlaqqa's response to the strike, or has a rival NRE such as Tsathoggua moved into the empty niche?

Byrd, who had narrowly survived an encounter with an unknown Mythos presence on his second Antarctic sojourn in 1934, eagerly added his voice to Ropes'. Forrestal reluctantly approved a series of expeditions designed to help manage the potential threat posed by NREs at both poles.

Operation Nanook

In late July 1946, the *Balao*-class submarine *USS Atule,* the US Coast Guard icebreaker *USCGC Northwind,* and three US Navy auxiliary ships led by the seaplane tender *USS Norton Sound,* arrived in Greenland's North Star Bay on

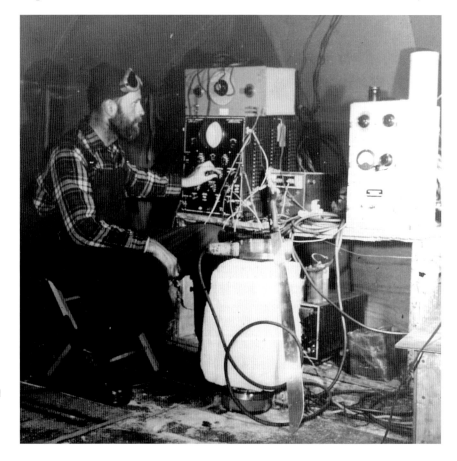

The US Antarctic Program photo library describes this picture as one of Albert H. Taylor (1879–1961) of the Naval Research Laboratory experimenting with sound transmission through ice at the Little America station during Operation *Highjump* in 1946–47. The man depicted looks considerably younger than the 67-year-old Taylor, however, and this may be a photo of Commander James Starkweather (1894–1973) using experimental radars designed by Taylor to detect Megarkaruan structures under the ice cap. (LOC)

On March 5, 1927, President Coolidge awarded Commander Richard E. Byrd (1888-1957) the Medal of Honor for his pioneering flight over the North Pole on May 9, 1926. The hand-written sextant readings in Byrd's journal of that flight do not match his typed dead-reckoning numbers, which historians take to be a sign of exhaustion, error, or fraud. Another possibility is that Byrd encountered (or entered geometric space distorted by) Itlaqqa, a Flying Polyp, or a similar NRE -- which would explain his decades-long, near-fanatical devotion to exploring Mythos activity in Antarctica. (LOC)

a supposedly cartographic mission, codenamed Operation *Nanook*. All but one of the ships had seen service in the Pacific Theater, with veteran crews who had survived combat operations in or near presumed NRE strongholds. Over the course of several weeks, the fleet surveyed the region for an area suitable for the establishment of a weather station and an airstrip suitable for launching combat and surveillance operations into Greenland's interior; by early August three Martin PBM Mariner bombers had delivered over 30,000 pounds of conventional ordnance over at least one Inuit village, as well as an isolated peak believed to be identifiable with the Hyperborean Mount Voormithadreth alluded to in both the *Pnakotika* and the pre-Roman *Book of Eibon*.

When one of the bombers crashed into the Fenris glacier after clipping an invisible object on its way back to the fleet's operating base near Thule, the *Norton Sound* contacted Danish authorities in an attempt to organize an overland rescue expedition. Although three Inuit tribes initially volunteered to assist the task force in recovering the downed crew, they balked and refused to proceed when they learned the plane's estimated location. The Inuit warned the Naval personnel that the territory was considered sacred to the evil spirit they called *Itlaqqa*, a name possibly derived from the Inuktun *Itla-shua* or Tunumiisut *Tlam-shua* ("Universe Owner"). The Inuits' description of this being suggested a possible connection to the Ojibwa and Cree cannibal madness-spirit *Witiko* or *Wendigo,* a supposition lent greater credence by the state in which the downed crew was eventually found: although they had evidently survived the crash itself, they murdered each other while awaiting rescue. The last to die had eaten the feet and hands of those who had preceded him in death, even though the plane's emergency food rations were found accessible and intact.

Operation Highjump

> *"The fantastic speed with which the world is shrinking ... is one of the most important lessons learned during [our] recent Antarctic exploration. I have to warn my compatriots that the time has ended when we were able to take refuge in our isolation and rely on the certainty that the distances, the oceans, and the poles were a guarantee of safety."*
>
> –Rear Admiral Richard Byrd (Ret.), after Operation *Highjump*

During Operation *Nanook*, in late August 1946, Rear Admiral Richard Cruzen led a separate and much larger expedition to Antarctica, codenamed Operation *Highjump*, with Byrd along as an "advisor." *Highjump's* Task Force 68 (TF 68) included more than 4,700 men, 33 aircraft, and 13 ships organized into three semi-independent groups, led by the newly built *Essex*-class aircraft carrier USS *Philippine Sea*, which would see its first combat action during the operation. Officially, the expedition was engaged in a scientific survey of the Antarctic coast that was to end in the establishment of a research base informally named "Little America IV."

(OPPOSITE)

On December 30, 1946, the Balao-class submarine USS *Sennet* rendezvoused with the Central Group of TF 68 off Scott Island, about 300 miles from the Antarctic coast. Its hydrophones had detected unusual activity beneath the Ross Sea ice. Rear Admiral Cruzen, on board the amphibious command ship USS *Mount Olympus*, ordered a reconnaissance in force by the *Sennet* as the icebreaker USCGC *Northwind* escorted the remainder of Central Group through the ice. Dr Waldo Lyon, an expert in acoustic physics and ice formation, boarded the *Sennet* along with Commander James Starkweather, a veteran of the 1933–34 Second Miskatonic Antarctic Expedition and ONI B-8 operative.

The *Sennet* encountered telepathic Megarkaruan opposition almost at once, but quick and humane disciplinary measures by Captain Joseph B. Icenhower contained the problem. (Dr Lyon also obtained valuable hydrophone readings that enabled later CIA work on human telepathy and mind-control in projects *Bluebird*, *Artichoke*, and MK *Ultra*.) On January 2, 1947, the *Sennet* positioned itself directly over the Megarkaruan city, pinpointing the few sound-emitting locations in the undersea near-necropolis. The city apparently hosted a shoggoth breeding pit, and launched at least three of the ancient bioweapons to destroy or drive off the *Sennet*. Shown here, the *Sennet* launches the third and fatal M28 HBX torpedo at nearly point-blank range, which disintegrated the attacker. With two more beasts incoming and the hydrophone showing no diminution in the supposedly destroyed shoggoth's signaling activity, and only seven torpedoes remaining in its arsenal, the *Sennet* retreated with severe bow damage. The *Northwind* towed the *Sennet* back to Scott Island the next day. Direct or indirect shoggoth attack (the logs refer to unusual, even impossible, movement of icebergs into the ships' path) also damaged the *Mount Olympus* and *Northwind*, and the cargo ships USS *Merrick* and USS *Yancey*. Reinforcement from the aircraft carrier *Philippine Sea*, which dropped salvoes of depth charges from its R4D Skytrain transports, suppressed Megarkarua activity against Central Group.

A rare photograph of a Mi-Gö in flight, shot from a B-17 gun camera over Germany in August 1944. Normal film cannot record Mi-Gö matter, likely due to its divergent superstring weft; the white dome in this shot may be a Yuggothian vehicle carapace, or the sunlight glinting off the Mi-Gö body. The USAAF classified all such sightings as "foo fighters," a name of uncertain origin. It may have come from men of the 415th Night Fighter Squadron overhearing Unit 10 agents referring to "Cthulhu" while investigating the sightings: "thooloo" or "thoo" lights becoming "foo fighters" in the official records due to phoneme drift or Unit 10 censorship. (Mary Evans Picture Library / Alamy)

Since at least the 1960s, conspiracy theorists have suggested that the true purpose of *Highjump* was an attack on a secret Nazi UFO base hidden beneath the Antarctic ice that served as a final redoubt for the defeated Reich. This is, of course, absurd. The true purpose of the mission was to establish a permanent American foothold on the continent that would allow it to surveil, and if necessary destroy, the ancient *Megarkarua sapiens* city that the Byrd and Pabodie expeditions had discovered in 1929 and 1931.

Byrd's previous expeditions had been greatly publicized in the United States, but he had studiously avoided any references to NRE phenomena in public statements about his experiences. As TF 68 approached the Antarctic coast, he revealed the true nature of the danger in a classified briefing aboard the *Philippine Sea*. While the few aerial photographs of the above-ground city in the Transantarctic Mountains strongly suggested that it was uninhabited, the *Balao*-class submarine USS *Sennet* located a second pre-human city on the sea floor beneath the Ross Ice Shelf in early September.

Over the next five months, TF 68 meticulously mapped numerous Mythos sites on the continent, frequently encountering Mi-Gö "foo fighter" probes. In December, efforts to establish a more permanent forward operating base carved into the thick ice of the West Antarctic Ice Sheet led to the inadvertent discovery of a massive temple complex, apparently wholly separate from the Megarkarua city, which was filled with sinister carvings of cyclopean bird-like saurians vaguely resembling pterodactyls: likely identifiable with the "Shantak-birds" mentioned in von Junzt's *Unaussprechlichen Kulten*. The collapsing ice freed several of these evidently ageless creatures, which harassed *Highjump* personnel for almost two weeks until shot down by F8F Bearcat fighters launched from the *Philippine Sea*. Despite these difficulties, by January 1947 *Highjump* had secured photographs, artifacts, and in several cases tissue samples from each of the pre-human sites they identified, as well as complete live (if hibernating) specimens of the Megarkarua themselves.

Victory had not come without cost. An extraordinarily high percentage of the men who had served in either polar theater began displaying symptoms of psychiatric disorders even before the mission ended. In *On the Ice*, a 1995 study focused on personnel stationed in the Antarctic over the previous 50 years, Dr Lawrence Palinkas determined that more than 5 percent of those who had spent time on the continent were experiencing symptoms "severe enough to warrant clinical intervention" after only a few months in theater. Even in those not struggling with the sudden and inexplicable onset of mental illness, Palinkas observed a drastic increase in antisocial behaviors, as time on the site magnified "seemingly trivial events and symptoms, transforming what would be viewed as mundane or unimportant in any other environment into something that is problematic and significant under conditions of isolation and confinement" – to say nothing of exposure to the frankly alien.

MAJIC and the Atomic Age

Success against the stiff resistance from NRE-associated forces in both polar regions had not only demonstrated that the United States could credibly combat Mythos entities in their own domains, but also proved the absolute

The destroyer USS *Jenkins* (DD-447) off California in January 1944. Prior to its role in Operation *Starfish Prime* (p. 57), *Jenkins* provided shore support and operational facilities for the Unit 10 detachments in the Philippines from February to April 1945. The Iranun people, traditional sailors and pirates, formed part of the "Moro" resistance to US occupation (1899-1913); certain Iranun villages rebelled again in February 1925 during the R'lyeh aftershock. Unit 10 raided and cleared those villages, killing a breeding population of Deep Ones and hybrids but never finding the cult center of Aira, the so-called Bandar Marmar Zamrud ('city of marble and beryl'). On Walpurgisnacht 1945, an unknown sub-oceanic force attacked *Jenkins* near Tarakan Island; the destroyer survived, and official Navy records blamed the damage on a mine. (LOC)

necessity of a more permanent and comprehensive management of the Cthulhu Wars. Secretary of the Navy James Forrestal made unified operations against the Mythos threat a condition of his becoming the United States' first Secretary of Defense.

In response to Forrestal's concerns, President Harry S. Truman signed Executive Order 9887 on August 22, 1947, "Designating Public Organizations Entitled to Enjoy Certain Privileges, Exemptions, and Immunities." This apparently innocuous document formally established a secret joint military/civilian Multi-Agency Joint Intelligence Command (MAJIC) in a classified annex. The new agency was authorized to use any and all means necessary to combat the NRE threat both at home and abroad.

As MAJIC's first director, Dr Curtis V. Ropes reunited the scattered former elements of the old Unit 10. At the prompting of a formal advisory committee of 12 prominent figures drawn from the military, intelligence, and academic communities, MAJIC moved quickly to establish global intelligence and communication networks to monitor known hotbeds of Mythos activities, with manned short-wave radio stations transmitting signals encoded in series of apparently random numbers. With the launch of the Russian *Sputnik* satellite in 1957 after several Mi-Gö encounters in the Soviet Union, it became clear to MAJIC that terrestrial surveillance would not be enough. By March 1958, the United States had placed two of its own artificial satellites in orbit, confirming the presence of a belt of protective radiation surrounding the planet, and coincidentally discovering an elder race of half-polypous, semi-material, and utterly alien entities that seemed to live within it, flitting between the upper atmosphere and outer space.

(OPPOSITE)

The MAJIC after-action assessment of *Starfish Prime* holds that the creature destroyed by the nuclear explosion at 11.00pm Honolulu time, July 8, 1962, was likely not the actual entity known as Cthulhu, but one of his spawn or kindred. (A recent reassessment posits that it was indeed Cthulhu, but as with the 1925 *Alert* encounter, he recovered.) Similar controversies extend to almost every aspect of the operation: eyewitness testimony frequently contradicts not only that of sailors or observers on the same deck, but even itself. Almost two-thirds of listed observers report a "second missile" and a second detonation seconds after the first, despite the impossibility of a second launch from Johnston Atoll. The USS *Halibut* was on Pacific patrol at the time, and may have launched a Regulus nuclear cruise missile on Commander W. R. Cobean's own recognizance upon encountering the Cthulhu-spawn. If so, MAJIC and the Pentagon understandably suppressed the evidence of a freelance nuclear release and redacted it even from internal reports. The official version puts "second missile" reports down to NRE time dilation or post-traumatic hysteria.

This view correlates reports from the deck of the helicopter carrier USS *Iwo Jima*, including the "second missile." A Bell UH-1 deploys a sensor array, repurposed from *Dominic* to MAJIC requirements. A destroyer screen (from left to right, USS *Newell*, USS *John S. McCain*, USS *O'Bannon*) lays down a torpedo and artillery barrage that slows, but does not halt, the Thing's advance.

THE VELA INCIDENT

On September 22, 1979, an American *Vela Hotel* satellite monitoring nuclear treaty compliance detected two rapid flashes of light – typically characteristic of a nuclear detonation – between the Prince Edward and Crozet islands in the South Indian Ocean. Although no nation has ever claimed responsibility for the detonation, the prevailing view of the US intelligence community identified it as a joint South African-Israeli nuclear weapons test. MAJIC files support this attribution, but notes that the blast occurred near the assessed location of a large Megarkarua colony believed to contain the largest shoggoth breeding pits outside Lake Vostok in Antarctica.

Operation Argus

Upon receiving a detailed brief from MAJIC indicating that these were the flying polyps described in the *Pnakotika* and the recovered Megarkaruan art and records and that they could represent a grave threat to American national security to which the United States could not credibly respond, President Dwight D. Eisenhower authorized a nuclear first strike against them. From August 27 to September 6, 1958, the USS *Norton Sound,* once more called into anti-Mythos duty, launched three modified X-171A missiles topped with 1.7-kiloton nuclear warheads into the upper atmosphere with assistance from nine other vessels outfitted with special radars and targeting suites. The detonations – at 100, 310, and 490 miles above sea level – each targeted dense pockets of flying polyp activity, destroying many of the alien creatures and creating rings of ionized energy meant to prevent them from counter-attacking the Earth's surface. The attack, dubbed Operation *Argus,* was publicly billed as a scientific exercise, a cover that had served MAJIC's predecessor agencies well ten years before.

Hartwell and Starfish

The sudden and unexpected discovery of NREs in the upper atmosphere also raised MAJIC's level of concern regarding activity in the inaccessible depths of the world's oceans. In 1949, the Department of Defense began development of a permanent sound surveillance system (SOSUS): effectively a net of hydrographic sensors designed to detect Soviet submarine activity transiting the corridor between the United Kingdom, Iceland, and Greenland. As early as 1955, MAJIC had indoctrinated several key staff members, and the program, codenamed Project *Hartwell*, was first tested near a Deep One settlement southwest of Bermuda in 1960. When tuned properly, SOSUS could warn of significant shoggoth activity as well as Soviet submarines, and if necessary detect the movements of other undersea entities. Fully operational in 1961, MAJIC's investment in *Hartwell* paid off almost immediately.

Hartwell detected significant sub-oceanic activity in the R'lyeh region on June 19, 1962, prompting an immediate response from MAJIC. By 10.00pm that day, MAJIC agents had landed on the amphibious assault ship USS *Iwo Jima*

The USS *New Jersey*, shown here conducting shore bombardment during the Korean War, served in at least three (and possibly many more) anti-Mythos operations during its 22 years in service. On April 30, 1944, she (along with the USS *Iowa* and USS *Massachusetts*) composed Bombardment Unit Zero, targeting known NRE-active sites near Nan Madol on Ponape before the main shelling began the next day. While decommissioned at the Atlantic Reserve Fleet yard in Bayonne, New Jersey, she served as the impromptu headquarters and prison facility for a 1949 MAJIC investigation (Operation *Festival*) of a subterranean worm-cult, conventional land structures being deemed too vulnerable to literal subversion. On October 31, 1968, *New* Jersey's 16in guns obliterated a Cham fishing village on the island of Hòn Mò that MAJIC suspected of being a Deep One outpost, an "Indochina Innsmouth" as Special Forces Colonel Kenton Stanfield put it. (PD)

and commandeered Joint Task Force 8 (JTF 8), a US Navy flotilla conducting the ongoing (since April) Operation *Dominic* high-altitude nuclear tests. The agents carried presidential authorization to use any and all means to respond – including, if necessary, the use of two Thor intermediate-range ballistic missiles, based on Johnston Atoll and carrying 1.4-megaton yield W49 nuclear warheads. A destroyer assigned to JTF 8, the USS *Jenkins*, made first contact with the enemy, firing a volley of torpedoes at one of Cthulhu's enormous spawn on June 20.

The first Thor nuclear strike failed: whether the rocket or the warhead malfunctioned or missed, or was somehow neutralized, remains highly classified, along with everything else about the test later codenamed *Starfish Prime*. Several other vessels became engaged in a running battle over the next two weeks, firing on the creature and then pulling back to slowly draw it into almost point-blank range for the single Thor nuclear missile that remained between the titanic demigod and the Hawaiian islands. On July 8, the *Iwo Jima* sighted the enemy less than 200 miles from the Johnston Atoll and ordered a second missile launch. This time, the warhead detonated successfully, disintegrating the nameless sky-spawn. The United States had once more exercised its nuclear first-strike policy against the Mythos.

The Mi-Gö Offensive

While the United States mounted an active nuclear offensive against Mythos entities, the more conventional battles in the conflict were almost categorically defensive. As MAJIC executed strikes against Megarkarua, Deep Ones, and flying polyps, Mi-Gö activity increased in multiple theaters, but did not take on a belligerent character immediately.

Mi-Gö had shadowed Allied and Axis aircraft throughout World War II without taking action against either side, suggesting that they intended to remain neutral, both in purely human conflicts and perhaps also in humanity's conflicts with its ancient predecessors. However, the Mi-Gö did upgrade their presence from the small glowing "foo fighters" (possibly the Mi-Gö themselves) to biometallic craft built on quasi-Euclidean discoid and conic lines. First sighted by civilian pilot Kenneth Arnold over Mt. Rainier, Washington on June 24, 1947, and then recovered by the US Army Air Force after a serendipitous lightning strike over Roswell, New Mexico the following month, these "flying saucers" characterized Mi-Gö activity for the rest of the century.

Korea, 1951

On April 10, 1951, a Mi-Gö flying disc launched from a mining base hidden in Korea's Masikyrong Mountains attacked a US Army infantry company in the so-called "Iron Triangle" near Chorwan after hovering over the battlefield and weathering artillery and small-arms fire for the better part of an hour. The craft swept the US position with an energy ray that incapacitated the entire company without killing any of the American troops. The targeted men displayed striated patterns of second- and third-degree burns accompanied by drastically elevated white blood cell counts, and experienced episodes of disorientation and memory loss for the rest of their lives.

Alaska, 1951

Three-and-a-half weeks later, a Canadian Pacific Airlines DC-4, on a scheduled flight for the United Nations from Vancouver to Tokyo via Anchorage, went off-course after reporting contact with a disc-shaped craft. The plane, registered as CF-CPC, made a final radio transmission near Mt. McKinley (known today as Denali), and then disappeared without a trace, taking 31 passengers with it. In 1993, MAJIC discovered a subterranean Mi-Gö base codenamed "Black Pyramid" only 8 miles from the point where contact with the aircraft had been lost.

Washington, 1952

Perhaps as an additional show of force, seven large Mi-Gö saucers hovered over Washington, DC, intermittently for almost two weeks in July 1952. On the night of July 19, the craft took up a low observational position over both the White House and the US Capitol. By July 29, President Truman

ordered the Air Force to prepare sorties to shoot down the saucers if and when they reappeared, despite MAJIC's caution that the Mi-Gö response to such provocation could not be anticipated because of their seemingly incomprehensible strategic doctrine. Those consequences ultimately went unexplored: by the time the Air Force was ready to deploy fighters in defense of the capital, the Mi-Gö had simply left the area.

Mythos Proxies

"Should the central government successfully use occult methods to defeat a movement based upon such methods, the very concepts of sorcery and magic which lend impetus to the insurgencies of the moment may gain strength and acquire even greater trouble-making potential for the future. In other words, the more successful the counterinsurgency campaign, if that campaign is based upon a counter-magic approach, the more ominous the outlook for the future."

–James R. Price & Paul Jureidini, Report to the Special Operations Research Office

While MAJIC focused on eliminating or at least mitigating the NRE threat, other agencies within the American security establishment sought to turn the powerful alien beings of the Alhazredic Mythos into instruments of statecraft. The Central Intelligence Agency (CIA), born like MAJIC from the remnants of the wartime OSS in 1947, resented MAJIC's primacy in occult

Soldiers of the US 2nd Infantry Division hunker down during an artillery barrage near Hwasun, South Korea, in October 1950. Their unit assisted the ROK 20th Regiment, 11th Division in counter-guerrilla operations in the hills, where remnants of the North Korean Army radicalized the so-called *Olaegodae* ("very old") mountain folk. The guerrillas and Olaegodae surprised the 5th Battalion of the 20th Regiment in an ambush near Hwasun in late October and wiped it out nearly to the last man. One surviving US soldier, L. C. Rufus, described "an ice-cold wind that seemed to be alive" choosing victims and dragging them off: unknown Mythos magic, Wendigo attack, or action by Itlaqqa or Hastur perhaps. The South Korean government exterminated the Olaegodae in the pacification campaign of 1951–52. (LOC)

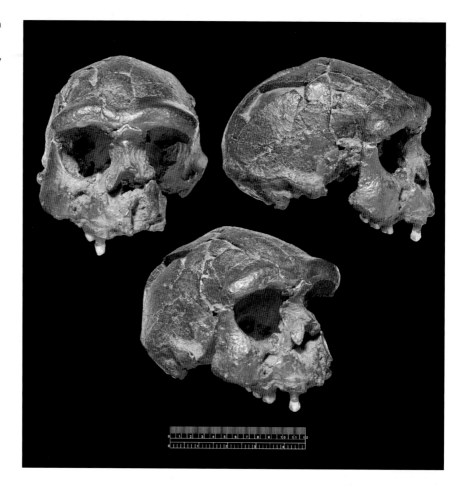

Reconstructed skulls of Java Man (Homo erectus) based on fossils (1.6 MYA) discovered at Sangiran, Java by G. H. R. von Koenigswald in 1936–41. Note the large, prominent incisors. (The Naturl History Museum / Alamy)

war planning. On the thin grounds that MAJIC's remit only covered counter-Mythos work, the CIA rapidly established its own occult operations shop, run out of the Technical Services Section under Dr Sidney Gottlieb. An expert in poisons and hypnosis known to his colleagues as "the black sorcerer," Gottlieb had obtained a cache of 1st-century Aramaic scrolls delivered to the CIA's Damascus Station by an Egyptian merchant in 1947. This *Damascus Codex* became the CIA's operational bible: their tame Whittemore Group analysts concluded that these scrolls provided NRE control mechanisms.

Tibet

Between 1951 and 1965, CIA's Special Activities Division trained and supplied several Tibetan volunteer paramilitary forces to resist occupation from Communist China. When a briefly successful uprising in Lhasa provoked an overwhelming Chinese military response in 1959, the CIA initiated an indirect counterattack.

On November 23, a small unit of Tibetan *Chushi Gangdruk* rebels led by two CIA officers entered a network of caves in Nepal providing access to an isolated portion of the Ü-Tsang Plateau in Tibet. Their mission was to locate

THREAT REPORT: PRE-HUMANS

"The new dates from Ngandong and Sambungmacan are surprisingly young and, if proven correct, imply that H. erectus persisted much longer in Southeast Asia than elsewhere in the world."
—Swisher, Rink, et al. "Latest Homo erectus of Java,"
Science 1996 Dec 13; 274:1870–4.

The *Pnakotic Manuscripts* maintain that the Earth has hosted, or will host, no fewer than 13 sentient species from the crinoid Megarkarua to two arthropod races (coleopterans and then arachnids) that are destined to succeed humanity. The humanoid species that currently share the surface with mankind are, for the most part, pre-human, although Miskatonic University scholars debate some details. Evolutionary competition with *Homo sapiens* has forced them into fringe environments: deep caves; remote islands; mountains; and rain forests.

Paleontologists and occultists working under MAJIC have identified four of these species with significant populations. Given the anomalously long lifespans of many NRE species, even an isolated colony might well be self-sustaining or even capable of demographic breakout if the human pressure were removed.

Parviraptor valusiani: Called the "serpent folk" in von Junzt's *Unaussprechlichen Kulten,* this intelligent bipedal species probably originated at some time in the Jurassic Period, or even as early as the Permian. By the Cenozoic Era, their population had been severely depleted, either by wars with other species, or by some global mass extinction event. Master sorcerers and poisoners, they primarily pose an intelligence threat – their ability to shape-shift and to teratogenically "morph" or remold humans has triggered at least one MAJIC mole hunt.

Gigantopithecus lemuriensis: Part of the genus *Gigantopithecus* which evolved in South Asia roughly 9 million years ago, *G. lemuriensis* stands 3m tall and weighs 540kg. Their name derives from the lost continent of Lemuria, where they either ruled or served as the warrior caste until its destruction around 400,000 years ago. Their psionic powers still conceal their ancient city of Shamballah somewhere in the Gobi Desert – the US Military Mission to Mongolia has one MAJIC-cleared NCO, but projecting force in this tense region between China and Russia remains difficult.

Homo hirsutus: This furry hominid species (called the Voormii in the *Book of Eibon*) evolved in the Pliocene (ca. 3.5 MYA), establishing a roughly Bronze Age-level of civilization in Greenland during the Bramertonian Interglacial Stage about 1 MYA. The return of the ice and a civil war between worshippers of Tsathoggua and Itlaqqa destroyed the Voormii civilization; they mostly survive as primitive remnants in the Himalayas (yeti), Caucasus and Pamir (almas), and the Pacific Northwest (sasquatch). Unless a given *H. hirsutus* actively serves an NRE, it poses little strategic threat, although troops of almas have badly mauled unprepared patrols in Afghanistan (both Russian and NATO) and Chechnya.

Homo erectus malevolens: Descended from the hominid species dubbed Java Man, *H. erectus malevolens* is better known as the Tcho-Tcho (from the Yi word meaning "to eat"). Tcho-Tcho tribes survive and even thrive in the military chaos of the Cambodian, Burmese, and Malaysian interior. Chinese intelligence indicates that Tcho-Tcho also survive in Tibet. Cannibal worshipers of the Twin Obscenity Nug–Yeb, the Tcho-Tcho show an almost innate talent for irregular warfare.

Only *H. erectus malevolens* maintains any real military presence, and with the destruction of the buried city of Alaozar in 1905, even they present no direct threat to humanity or the United States. That said, none of these species has any great reason to be fond of their *H. sapiens* successors, and the *Necronomicon* and *Book of Eibon* state that individuals of all species are capable of sorcery. When a single wizard can potentially manifest the equivalent of a gigaton nuclear strike, the only true safety may lie in the complete extinction of these pre-human races.

and awaken an NRE worshiped locally as the deity Tsaugnar Fon, which they believed would attack Chinese troops when it emerged.

The entire unit went missing, and both CIA officers were declared dead in 1960. However, in 1981 two men claiming to be those same CIA officers were captured by the People's Liberation Army in China's Yunnan province. Turned over to the United States after two years of interrogation, both men claimed that they had been in the mountains for less than 11 days when they were captured.

Congo

When the Democratic Republic of Congo (later Zaire) achieved independence from Belgium in 1960 and installed a left-leaning prime minister, the CIA and Belgium's General Intelligence and Security Service (SGRS) cooperated closely to prevent a feared Communist takeover. While the Belgians backed an authoritarian military coup led by Joseph Mobutu in 1961, the CIA instead recruited assets from among an underground NRE cult, the Army of Holy Temperance Unleashed (AHTU).

Headquartered in a long-abandoned temple complex first described in 1765 by the British explorer Sir Wade Jermyn, the AHTU raided Cuban and other Communist outposts with troops of killer white apes. While initially effective, the AHTU proved more interested in nihilistic violence than in the agendas of either Mobutu or the United States.

Vietnam

Beginning in 1961, The CIA recruited, supplied, and trained battalions

(OPPOSITE)

Recon Team (RT) Rhode Island served as the main MAJIC strike force within the Military Assistance Command, Vietnam – Studies and Observation Group (MACV-SOG). By August 1968 and the launch of the Operation *Bulldog* strikes against Tcho-Tcho ritual sites in Cambodia, MAJIC theoretically had full CIA cooperation and planning assistance, which in practice meant strategic paralysis and a piecemeal approach to anti-Tcho-Tcho operations. This August 13 mission in Kampong Cham exemplifies these weaknesses: a "heavy" RT of 12 men inserted into a Neolithic Mimotien ruin, a target identified from sensor overflights without on-site intelligence of any kind, as RT Rhode Island's indigenous Hmong fighters unanimously disavowed any knowledge of such a place.

The Tcho-Tcho attack the Mimotien "ring" earthwork, supported by a Mythos entity known as the "Swimmer in Darkness" – possibly a form of Flying Polyp, or the formless spawn of a local NRE such as Nug-Yeb or Sau-gaja (the "elephant of Saturn"). The Tcho-Tcho use blowguns and sacred bronze swords in this attack, although they eagerly used M16s and other American-supplied arms elsewhere in Indochina. This apparently ritual requirement saved the life of the three men (Special Forces Staff Sergeant Omar Crawford and two Hmong commandos) manning the machine gun in the (entirely unrecorded) temple ruin overlooking the site. They held off the Tcho-Tcho all night, destroyed as much of the ring and temple as practicable at dawn, and were exfiltrated by helicopter.

from several Indochinese indigenous peoples for paramilitary warfare against the Viet Cong, the North Vietnamese Army, and allied Communist forces. The Tcho-Tcho *"Armée Inconnu"* rapidly slipped the CIA leash and by 1968 had revealed themselves as a threat to the stability of South Vietnam – and the US presence in the country – equal to the Communist North.

After supposedly friendly Tcho-Tcho ambushed, killed, and then ate a US Army patrol, the US responded by bombing several religious sites considered holy to their obscene twin cannibal deities Nug and Yeb. These raids were followed up by Operation *Bulldog,* a series of punitive ground attacks against Tcho-Tcho settlements in Cambodia in August 1968. Although the Green Berets inflicted serious casualties on the Tcho-Tcho, their priests' ability to summon and control several kinds of lesser NREs – including at least one creature described in intelligence after-action reporting only as an "oblong swimmer in darkness" (possibly a terrestrial sub-species of the flying polyps) – forced the US to airlift its few surviving troops out of harm's way only a few weeks into the campaign.

Nicaragua

In 1987, the CIA began an operation to awaken Qol'corotz, a sinister, black-winged, toad-like NRE, to assist the Nicaraguan Contras in overthrowing the leftist Sandinista regime. Satellite imagery had located a site believed to be the legendary pre-Mayan "Temple of the Toad" in Honduras, not far from a Contra camp on the Nicaraguan border. Rather than risking American lives in the attempt to rouse the slumbering deity, CIA operatives supplied the Contras with several incantations from the Projekt *Leo* copy of *Unaussprechlichen Kulten* smuggled out of East Berlin in 1961.

The Contras had apparently unleashed something by March 13, 1988, but once more it proved uncontrollable, rampaging through the Honduras-Nicaragua border region for five days before a rapidly deployed US airborne force drove the unidentified creature back into hiding.

Other Operations

Not every occult CIA mission ended in disaster, at least not immediately. CIA assets among the Kheshthaogha-worshippers in western Iran aided the overthrow of Prime Minister Mossadegh in 1953, and CIA assets used a hyperspace "tunnel of Nyogtha" to move between West and East Berlin for most of the Cold War. The CIA also traced Czechoslovakian support for the Starry Wisdom "urban guerrilla movement" in the 1970s. Starry Wisdom had a distressing ability to locate and bomb MAJIC safe houses and black sites, although its motives for the November 1970 bombing of the bronze replica of the Liberty Bell in Portland, Oregon remain murky. CIA remote viewers also uncovered the identity of the terrorist who assassinated an Israeli NRE expert posted in Washington to liaise with MAJIC in June 1973.

A CIA Snake Hunt

The vulnerabilities of the CIA's NRE program were not limited to foreign intervention. MAJIC agent Felix Ritter, temporarily detailed to the CIA in order to support the agency's Project *Artichoke* mind-control program, identified a potential mole within the CIA's ranks in 1971. In November 1970, during a briefing on the progress of Project *Often* – meant to harness black magic and "the forces of darkness [to] challenge the concept that the inner reaches of the mind are beyond reach" – Ritter noted several references to incantations, spells, and entities that did not come from the CIA's limited library of NRE-related material. At first suspecting a leak within MAJIC, Ritter eventually concluded that at least one key member of the CIA team had gained separate and extensive access to a vast library of original and complete Alhazredic documents.

Threatened with losing the whole NRE program, CIA counterintelligence officials mounted an extensive investigation into Project *Artichoke*. By early 1971, investigators had accrued enough odd and discomfiting evidence to reach a disturbing conclusion: at least one critical staff member was not actually human. The evidence, when shared with MAJIC, seemed to suggest that the group (and potentially the rest of the CIA) had been penetrated by one or more *Parviraptor valusiani,* the secretive "serpent folk" mentioned in von Junzt's *Unaussprechlichen Kulten*. Although the serpentine infiltrator or infiltrators were never formally identified, it may be significant that Dr Sidney Gottlieb suddenly retired in early 1972, just as the investigation was reaching its full swing.

THE GLOBAL WAR ON HORROR (1991–)

"What we may be witnessing is not just the end of the Cold War, or the passing of a particular period of postwar history, but the end of history as such."
—Francis Fukuyama, *The National Interest*

Specialists Van Kauran and Carter reconnoiter the slopes of Nanga Ranik near Nuriab during a MAJIC liaison mission with the local chief Amir Barzai Agah in Kunar Province, Afghanistan in 2009. (PD)

The ancient Near East was the cradle of civilization, with complex human cultures springing up for the first time thanks to the concurrent advent of urban settlements and writing. By the 4th millennium BC, Mesopotamian trading networks stretched from India to Spain, and the men of that epoch knew beyond the shadow of doubt that they were not alone in the world. They had, after all, built their civilizations on the ruins of cities built by older beings. But as the epochs passed, their heirs sought the favor of gods that their forebears had instead known to appease, bringing ruin upon their cities and settlements until at last their true nature was hidden or forgotten, with only a scattered few bearing the truth and the power that came with it.

Around 2600 BC, a secretive sect of priests founded temples on the banks of the Euphrates dedicated to the most powerful of these dreaming deities. As the old Assyrian Empire rose around them, the temples grew into cities. Both were called Tuttul, in honor of the god known to MAJIC as Cthulhu. The largest stood on the site of present-day Hit, Iraq until terrified invading Medes and Cimmerians burned it to the ground in 614 BC. The other (also dedicated to the god Dagan, or Dagon) still stands above a rocky Syrian village called Tell Bi'a, nine miles north of Ar-Raqqah. It is perhaps no coincidence that in the closing years of the 20th century, the United States found its security interests so closely tied to the stability of the old centers of NRE worship in the Middle East, Africa, and Southern Europe.

The HAARP facility in Gakona, Alaska. Although scheduled to be shut down in summer 2014 and then again in summer 2015, it remains open, officially under the control of the University of Alaska Fairbanks. (PD)

A New World Order

By the 1990s, Iraq had come to represent a particularly dangerous source of human-enabled NRE activity, with an increasingly isolated regime more than willing to employ Mythos weapons in the service of its national interests. During its long war with Iran, Saddam Hussein's Ba'ath regime had uncovered a prehistoric shoggoth left behind by Deep Ones in the Tigris delta. The Ba'athists deployed weaponized shoggoth quasi-matter against its own people at Qandil and Soka in 1985 and 1987, respectively, to quell local unrest. In addition, limited intelligence reporting suggested that teams of Iraqi

Pinched by shrinking defense and intelligence budgets, MAJIC had to partner with the Air Force, the Navy, and the Defense Advanced Research Projects Agency (DARPA) in order to construct the High Frequency Active Auroral Research Program (HAARP) in Alaska in 1993.

MAJIC intended to deploy this complex energy weapon terrestrially against Itlaqqa, and in the ionosphere against the flying polyps and the Mi-Gö. The additional requirements levied on the array by MAJIC's well-intentioned but unqualified partners lengthened the development cycle and left its core functionality weakened.

The first HAARP strike against Itlaqqa was worse than ineffectual, causing a major Arctic outbreak in early December 2000 that temporarily drew Itlaqqa to the north and west of the continental United States. Before a second, corrected test restrained the ancient being in the far north, confused civilian authorities fielded a flurry of murder cases involving cannibalism and a drastic uptick in *Homo hirsutus* activity in the same areas.

archaeologists working under Republican Guard command had uncovered several more lost Mythos sites – including the famed "city of the bells" of the daemon sultan Azathoth – that had the potential to significantly alter the regional balance of power.

MAJIC saw Iraq's invasion of Kuwait as an indication either that the regime believed other items or sites of power could be found in Kuwaiti territory, or that Saddam's magi believed they had already amassed enough power to ensure that a more aggressive regional policy could not be easily halted.

As a result, when the United States decided to intervene, specially trained teams of MAJIC officers embedded with infantry and armor units crossing into Iraq from Kuwait and Saudi Arabia in February 1991. MAJIC officers directed precision air strikes against half-excavated temple sites and ziggurats, and quietly removed stockpiles of ancient tablets, scrolls, and grimoires from underground bunkers while the "normal" war raged around them.

With the Soviet Union on the edge of collapse, MAJIC for the first time openly used weapons developed since the 1940s for a broader global war against a similarly armed superpower. They rooted serpent folk infiltrators working for Saddam out of coalition ranks using techniques developed during CIA snake hunts in the 1970s, neutralized Iraqi-bred shoggoths with repurposed Megarkaruan technology, and used electro-magnetic "keys" developed during MAJIC's study of the Mi-Gö to close toroidal stargates that the Iraqis had opened beneath ancient Uruk and Lagash.

Keeping the Peace

MAJIC's official support dwindled as the Pentagon mistakenly conflated the end of the Cold War with the end of the Cthulhu Wars. MAJIC officers operating alongside NATO forces in Bosnia and Herzegovina prevented a degenerate Serbian sect from sacrificing a squad of Polish UN peacekeepers

at an ancient black monolith in the ruins of Buŭim Castle in October 1995. Although the ritual failed, MAJIC nevertheless called in air strikes that failed to destroy the black stone, but badly damaged the ongoing peace talks. With no apparent ongoing threat, critics of MAJIC's extensive mandate suggested that the need for the special unit had passed.

By 1996, MAJIC would be forced to deploy to Liberia and Sierra Leone without official authorization, to combat resurgent cults of Azathoth, Hastur, and Nyarlathotep that had risen to limited power on the margins of the diamond-rich countries' civil wars. Declaring themselves priests of the true "traditional" indigenous religions, the cult leaders and false priests had urged warlords and desperate political leaders to perform human and child sacrifices to the "old gods" in exchange for invincibility in battle. Lacking official sanction and unable to oppose these cults openly, MAJIC instead used private military contracting as cover for their activities. They assassinated several key cult leaders, and intimidated several others into providing intelligence on regional cult activities and abandoning their bloodthirsty practices.

A grave complex from the megalithic El Infiernito site in Colombia, dated to ca. 900 BC. As a subterranean chamber, this site was likely dedicated to the Muisca god of floods, Chibchacum, imprisoned underground by the hero Bochica. Chibchacum may be the local representation of Cthulhu, who has a surprisingly strong cult presence in the Andes region. MAJIC private military contractors carried out an unknown mission at El Infiernito in 2006. (PD)

The Mullahs of Leng

The attacks against the World Trade Center and the Pentagon on September 11, 2001, quickly shifted the discussion among America's intelligentsia from governing a post-conflict world to aggressively stamping out global dangers, be they supernatural or mundane. For as much damage as the 9/11 attacks had done, high-level intelligence officials were understandably concerned that a similar terrorist group could do much greater damage to the American homeland using even poorly constructed Mythos weapons or partially controlled NREs. Consequently, MAJIC's decade-long decline was quickly and quietly reversed.

MAJIC officers were in Afghanistan as early as mid-October 2001, supporting CIA and US Special Forces operations on the ground and leading preemptive strikes against the NREs. Tribes of *H. erectus malevolens* and other unidentified near-human species who had lived in Afghanistan and Pakistan for centuries took advantage of the chaos to step up their predatory activities. Despite their often disturbing and heretical brands of Islam, the hardy tribes of the arid Leng Plateau in Afghanistan's Zabul province provided more than their share of terrorist recruits and guerrilla commanders, many of whom attempted to bring other non-human allies into the fight.

MAJIC officers provided special training to NATO troops operating in the sparsely populated agricultural districts in eastern Farah province in order to help them combat an ongoing infestation of aggressive Ghouls throughout

(OPPOSITE)

The district of Zin, in central Afghanistan between the Orzugan and Daykundi provinces, had been a no-go area for NATO forces since the invasion began. In 2006, a series of sweeps called Operation *Mountain Thrust* attempted to clear the Taliban out of the mountains with little success. MAJIC analysts noted the commonality of names with the "Azathoth-formed Vaults of Zin" supposedly tangent to the Serpent-folk realm of Yoth, the Dreamlands, and the Plateau of Leng. Further research, recon, and drone imagery pinpointed a pre-Islamic (possibly proto-Bönpa) temple on the slopes of Mount Leng-e Mulla Aman just northwest of Zin. When in 2007 intelligence chatter put the reclusive Mullah Dadullah Akhund Leng in Zin, MAJIC launched Operation *Mountain Hound* to kill the mullah and if possible shut down the hyperspace gateways to Zin from the temple.

On October 28, a large combined-arms assault closes in on the temple, unfortunately coinciding with a Mi-Gö embassy to the mullah. Supporting gunfire from the AC130U Spectre aircraft overhead warps and veers in non-Euclidean patterns consistent with previous reports from NRE-infested combat zones. Fire from the ground units is less distorted, but a gravitic interference pattern (the green glow on the ground, seen warping or shriveling soldiers caught inside the field effect) raised by the Lengi defenders saps its inertia and momentum. The short, vulpine, horned "Men of Leng" variously resemble Ghouls, Tcho-Tcho, and Serpent Folk, and may be a hybrid pre-human species. Rather than stop to overwhelm the Blackhawks, the Mi-Gö flew through the gunships and into the sky, escaping. The assault force killed a Mythos-wielding target presumed to be the Mullah of Leng and detonated its remaining heavy explosives inside the temple to unknown effect

A MAJIC operative (holding field-bound grimoire) with a US Army communications and coordination team on a rooftop in Hit, Iraq during Operation *River Blitz* in February 2005. In the chaotic conditions of the Iraq invasion, MAJIC had to keep its footprint light and agile, ready to move on any rumor of NRE activity or artifact discovery. The Cthulhu-cult leader and terrorist known as Zuti al-Tanzil operated out of Hit from 2002 to 2006; he (or a gem he looted from the Baghdad Museum known as the "Fire of Asshurbanipal") was likely the target for this particular raid. (PD)

2004 and 2005, likely summoned to the area by the syncretic "Mullahs" of Leng. The area, known for centuries as Gulistan, had to be pacified by Operation *Thurber,* a three-month campaign of air strikes beginning in January 2006.

In Operation *Mountain Hound* in October 2007, MAJIC and Special Forces killed the infamous Mullah Dadullah Akhund Leng outside a long-sealed pre-Islamic temple on the Pakistani border, 80 miles east of Kandahar. The strike came just as Dadullah was concluding an arrangement with a group of Mi-Gö who had operated in the area for centuries. Although several Mi-Gö were killed in the assault, no broader retaliation has occurred as yet.

The Coming Strange Times

Although not common, connections between "traditional" terrorist groups and NRE cults or beings had been unexpectedly frequent in Afghanistan, and by 2006 it was clear that this trend was not limited to central Asia. Even terrorist groups and separatist movements with no previous connection to NREs were being tracked to Mythos sites and found with Mythos documents, as if they were being deliberately encouraged and manipulated by an outside force.

After a failed attack against a Detroit-bound airliner on Christmas 2008 sponsored by al-Qaeda leaders in Yemen, a joint MAJIC–CIA team traced several terrorists from Indonesia, Pakistan, Iraq, Syria, Lebanon, Libya, and Mali to an established camp just outside the infamous Nameless City in the desert on the Saudi-Yemeni border. Here, signals intelligence (SIGINT) intercepts indicate the cell met with an individual they called Tawil al-ʿUmr (an Arabic *nom de guerre* roughly translated as the "most ancient and prolonged of life"). Facing what appeared to be a Mythos threat, MAJIC ordered a Predator strike from Camp Lemonnier in Djibouti, but by the time the drone reached its target, the meeting had ended and the attendees had scattered.

Interrogations of captured operatives who knew of the meeting, combined with seven years of closely analyzed SIGINT produced by MAJIC's Mythos analysis unit, suggest that key members of otherwise separate terrorist movements had agreed to a long-term strategy referred to only as Yajiʿu al-Shudhdhadh: "the coming strange times" or "the coming abnormal ones" (YaS in MAJIC jargon). This may be the original form of a term recorded in the Greek *Necronomicon* as *Iok Sotot* or *Yog-Sothoth*. The mysterious Tawil al-ʿUmr, in hiding after the failed 2008 drone strike, remains in command

Two MAJIC Special Forces operators in Yemen in 2013 hunt for al-Azredic carvings or bas-reliefs in an Abbasid-era ruin. Of the estimated 11,000 epigraphic inscriptions in southern Arabia, only a handful have ever been published or translated; much of MAJIC's Yemen mission simply consisted of photographing and mapping these carvings. (DOD)

THREAT REPORT: MI-GÖ

"The things come from another planet, being able to live in interstellar space and fly through it... They come here to get metals from mines that go deep under the hills, and I think I know where they come from. They will not hurt us if we let them alone, but no one can say what will happen if we get too curious about them. Of course a good army of men could wipe out their mining colony. That is what they are afraid of. But if that happened, more would come from outside – any number of them. They could easily conquer the earth, but have not tried so far because they have not needed to."

–Henry W. Akeley, letter to Professor Albert Wilmarth (May 5, 1928)

The utterly alien Mi-Gö rule a vast, ancient interstellar empire with outposts throughout the known Galaxy, and maintain a presence on at least three other planetary bodies in our solar system. Although the Mi-Gö have been on Earth for at least 130 million years, MAJIC assesses that there were fewer than 1,000 individual specimens on Earth as of early 2015. More significant populations are believed to reside on Mars, the Moon, and especially on Pluto, where they have erected massive black spires and pyramids that function as both living quarters and mineral processing facilities.

Mi-Gö range in length from 1.7 to 2.2m, with two large sets of crustacean-like grasping claws attached to a generally tubular body. Membranous dorsal wings serve to propel and maneuver the creatures in the vacuum of space. A wrinkled, ellipsoid head is topped with fleshy tentacles that sense a much wider spectrum of light than human sight can, and hear several lower registers of sound. Mi-Gö soft tissues are pink and spongiform, and due to a peculiarity of their alien composition they are impossible to capture on film. Electromagnetic interference emitted by the creatures hampers digital video and photography, but does not fully prevent it.

Because their wings provide only limited maneuverability in Earth's atmosphere, the Mi-Gö operate several classes of aircraft built along pseudo-Euclidean lines: glowing spheroid scouts, larger discoid multipurpose craft, and massive conoid "mother-ships" like those seen above Phoenix, Arizona, in 1997. Although wresting air superiority from the Mi-Gö has been a primary mission of numerous "skunk works" aircraft development programs since at least 1955, the US Air Force has been unable to demonstrate consistent success in air-to-air combat.

Mi-Gö outposts are typically situated in hilly or mountainous regions where they operate extensive mining outposts, sometimes digging miles below the surface to find veins of rare minerals which they apparently require for sustenance. In some cases, Mi-Gö excavations have revealed unstable rifts or gates that allow the Mi-Gö and specially prepared humans to travel to other planets, or even to separate universes vibrating at a different quantum frequency. While the minerals the Mi-Gö harvest hold no present strategic value to humans, the rifts (or more precisely, the NREs believed to be beyond them) represent a genuine danger to American national security.

The Mi-Gö attempt to avoid contact with humans whenever possible. In unavoidable or extreme situations, Mi-Gö surgically altered to approximate human appearance and speech recruit intermediaries from among nearby human populations, in a few cases forming long-term asset relationships with multiple generations of humans. The Mi-Gö reward successful agents with transhuman immortality, uploading the brain into a metallic cylinder complete with spider-like cybernetic limbs and broad-spectrum sensors.

Currently the Mi-Gö are not hostile if left to their own devices, but they will defend their bases vigorously if attacked. They hold no special affection for humanity, but seem uninterested in turning their impressive technological advantage toward our extermination. For now.

of the group, but communicates only by supernatural means to ensure his safety. The 2015 evacuation of American counterterrorist forces from Yemen following the Houthi rebel capture of Sana'a limits MAJIC intelligence and countermeasures against a Yog-Sothoth cult operating on the ground in al-Azrad's home city.

The Long War

Although the full scope of MAJIC's current operations is known only to a handful of high-ranking officials within the US intelligence community, the group almost certainly continues to operate alongside US special operations troops across the Middle East and North Africa. Facing a disparate threat and with ongoing requirements in at least two still-active war zones, MAJIC has been increasingly forced to work with, and through, local allies to confront NREs indirectly. Joint US-French counter-Mythos teams police the Mi-Gö haunted wastes of Niger and Northern Mali, while MAJIC trains national military units in countries as far apart as Tunisia and Mongolia to address, respectively, Deep One incursions from the Mediterranean and the ongoing threat presented by the city of Carcosa in the Gobi Desert.

The Islamic State of Iraq and Syria's (ISIS) assault on ancient archaeological sites across ancient Mesopotamia, and the resulting sale of thousands of only partially identified NRE artifacts, have forced MAJIC to launch a major

The General Atomics MQ-1C Gray Eagle unmanned aerial vehicle (UAV) has served a critical role in the United States anti-Mythos war in conflict zones across the globe since 2010. Named for the 19th-century Wichita shaman, the Gray Eagle is the only UAV in active service capable of fielding the *Antediluvian* anti-NRE sensor package as well as a full complement of air-to-ground weapon systems. MAJIC is believed to have at least 46 of these specially outfitted drones in operation as of late 2015, with most in active intelligence/surveillance/reconnaissance (ISR) missions. (DOD)

counter-proliferation mission in addition to its other commitments. Multiple reports indicate that the most significant items recovered from the deserts of Babylon and Sumer never enter the antiquities market, and are instead funneled into the hands of YaS soldiers to be used in future attacks.

More recent investigations have suggested that YaS may be funding "alternative worship" sites in several major US cities, whose doctrine bears a striking resemblance to the Cthulhu cult destroyed a century ago. There are also unconfirmed suspicions that the group was responsible for a major K'n-Yani mobilization below Texas in late 2014. MAJIC's counterattack, initially carried out under cover of the Special Forces exercise *Jade Helm*, is ongoing.

We can only hope that MAJIC will be ready when the next stage of the war begins.

SOURCES

When addressing a topic such as this one, with no authorized press releases, academic histories, or even large-scale journalistic efforts to rely on, putting this work together would have been impossible without personal communications and interviews. For the most part, I honor my sources' desire for (often insistence upon) anonymity and secrecy, but my primary source having passed on, I feel I owe it to his memory to thank Dr Ambrose Dexter for his assistance.

In October 2005, I was in Las Vegas on a technical writing assignment and found myself dining alone – or rather, waiting to dine alone – at the Golden Steer steakhouse. While at the bar, I struck up a conversation with a distinguished-looking, older gentleman with a very dark tan (I later heard him call it "my Los Alamos makeover") who introduced himself as "Ambrose Dexter." Perhaps it was the bourbon talking, but I responded with: "Just like in the Lovecraft story!" He admitted that yes, he had been one of Lovecraft's correspondents: an early science-fiction fan just getting his degree in metallurgy, fascinated by the visions he saw in those tales, and eager to share his knowledge of physics and chemistry with the master. Dexter told me Lovecraft had used his name in a story as a tip of the nib to his informative pen pal.

We dined together, the first of many such times as I traveled back and forth to Las Vegas, talking about Lovecraft, jazz horn players, military history and the current wars, and eventually his career. While Dr Dexter (he had several degrees, including one in Egyptology that he assured me was strictly honorary – he and Egyptian Antiquities Minister Dr Zahi Hawass had worked together on some NASA project, it emerged) was initially reserved, he unbent somewhat as we got to know each other better. I think he was lonely: he lived in a large house far out in the Nevada desert with only Bubastis, a mountain lion he'd raised from a cub, for company. (Animals loved him; coyotes constantly wandered onto the porch while we talked.) He strongly disapproved of the Bush administration, which may have eventually inspired him to do what he did. Also, he may have felt the end coming.

In late 2007, he gave me a large legal manila folder crammed with documents, memos, and his own research notes covering much of the subject matter of this book, especially the variously redirected nuclear tests. Even now, I think it unwise to reveal exactly how Dr Dexter obtained his information and exactly what he provided me, but I can say he had a hand in a great many nuclear and aerospace projects, both military and civilian, for the better part of five decades, and he had a wide range of correspondents and colleagues. I spent several years using the leads he gave me to further my own investigation into what I dubbed the Cthulhu Wars, always knowing that a quick email or phone call to him would inspire and advance the work.

One day in 2013 (he would have been at least 100 years old by then) his energies must have given out. My emails bounced, his phone number was apparently disconnected – we had avoided surface mail, of course, for years. No government contact I had would even admit that Dr Dexter had ever existed, much less that he had worked for the government, or that he had died. I sometimes still cannot believe that he has left us, preferring to picture him still living out there in the desert somewhere. I will always cherish his urging me to "reveal everything" and always remember his white grin gleaming in the dark of his back porch, where the night would turn his "atomic tan" to pure jet black as he reached down to let the wild animals lick his hands.

The occultist and anthropologist Friedrich Wilhelm von Junzt (1795–1840) compiled details of the cult worship and practices he encountered during his travels in Asia, Europe, and Latin America in his magnum opus *Unaussprechlichen Kulten* (Dusseldorf, 1839). The US government has acquired or destroyed all known copies as strategic resources. (Lee Mayer)

FURTHER READING, WATCHING, AND GAMING

H. P. Lovecraft

With Lovecraft's fiction in the public domain, it can easily be found on the Internet or in e-book form. S. T. Joshi's three-volume annotated edition of Lovecraft's fiction for Penguin Classics is probably the best version for completeness and textual accuracy.

Lovecraft's works most relevant to the Global War on Horror appear below. Since they have been variously reprinted over the years, they are dated by year of composition rather than publication.

"The Call of Cthulhu" (1926). The story that started the "Cthulhu Mythos." Vast narrative fugue comprises everything from the St. Bernard Parish raid to the global cult of Cthulhu and the Old Ones.

"Pickman's Model" (1926). Reveals the existence of the Ghoul warren beneath Boston.

The Case of Charles Dexter Ward (1927). Historical necromancy corrupting contemporary Providence, told within a bravura twinned-mystery structure.

"The Whisperer in Darkness" (1930). Establishes the Mi-Gö as an extraterrestrial threat in the paradigmatic story of alien persecution.

At the Mountains of Madness (1931). Record of the Miskatonic Antarctic Expedition describes what the survivors found there.

"The Shadow Over Innsmouth" (1931). Contains the report that led to the Innsmouth Raid and began the covert Cthulhu Wars.

Other Fiction

Bloch, Robert. *Strange Eons* (Pinnacle Books, Los Angeles, 1979). Presents a world of omnipresent cult activity that fulfills Lovecraft's predictive nightmares.

Derleth, August. "The Black Island" (*Weird Tales,* January 1952). Concludes with the atomic bombing of R'lyeh during a nuclear test.

Detwiller, Dennis. *Denied to the Enemy* (Tynes Cowan Corp., Seattle, 2003). World War II novel set in the *Delta Green* universe.

Johnson, Robert Barbour. "Far Below" (*Weird Tales,* June/July 1939). Unveils the secret war between the Ghouls and the Special Subway Detail of the NYPD.

Lumley, Brian. *The Burrowers Beneath* (DAW Books, New York, 1974). Over-the-top novel of a full secret-war mobilization against a Mythos threat, the "Cthonians."

Stross, Charlie. *The Atrocity Archives* (Golden Gryphon Press, Urbana, IL, 2004). This novel and its sequels combine Lovecraft with tradecraft; they're spy thrillers in a Mythos-haunted world.

Games

Delta Green (Pagan Publishing, 1997). By combining the national security state with the Cthulhu Mythos, this magnificent setting for the *Call of Cthulhu* tabletop role-playing game manages to encapsulate both paranoias. Coming soon as a standalone RPG from Arc Dream Publishing.

Hornet Leader: The Cthulhu Conflict (DVG, 2013). Expansion for tabletop carrier-mission sim *Hornet Leader* covers the War on Horror.

"The Raid on Innsmouth" (Chaosium, 1992). Brilliant RPG simulation of the titular raid, for *Call of Cthulhu.*

Strange Aeons (Uncle Mike's Worldwide, 2nd ed. 2015). Lovecraftian skirmish miniatures game; its 32mm figures are essentially compatible with Osprey's 28mm miniatures lines. The monsters should loom at least a little larger.

Movies

The Devil's Tomb (2009). Special Forces team in the Middle East encounters a primordial temple that serves as a prison for the Nephilim. Straight-to-DVD.

Monsters (2010). Director Gareth Edwards depicts a world halfway through an incomprehensible alien invasion from a civilian perspective behind the lines. His *Godzilla* (2014) foregrounds the military response to prehistoric demigods.

The Objective (2008). Crackling uncertainty horror follows a Special Forces team in Afghanistan; tightly scripted and directed by Daniel Myrick.

R-Point (2004). Kong Su-chang directs the best of the films mentioned here, about a South Korean platoon sent into a nightmarish rescue mission during the Vietnam War.

Ravenous (2002). Writer Ted Griffin infuses this cavalry vs Wendigo story set in the 1840s West with black humor and irony.